DOLLY
CITY ORLY CASTEL-BLOOM

TRANSLATED BY DALYA BILU
AFTERWORD BY KAREN GRUMBERG

DALKEY ARCHIVE PRESS / CHAMPAIGN AND LONDON

Originally published in Hebrew as *Dolly City* by Zmora Bitan, Tel Aviv, 1992
Copyright © by Orly Castel-Bloom and Hakibbutz Hameuchad Publishing House
Afterword copyright © 2010 by Karen Grumberg
English translation © by the Institute for the Translation of Hebrew Literature
Published by arrangement with the Institute for the Translation of Hebrew Literature
First U.S. edition, 2010

Library of Congress Cataloging-in-Publication Data

Castel-Bloom, Orly, 1960-
[Doli siti. English]
Dolly City / Orly Castel-Bloom ; translated by Dalya Bilu. -- 1st U.S. ed.
p. cm.
Originally published: Tel-Aviv : Zemorah-Bitan, 1992.
ISBN 978-1-56478-610-4 (pbk. : alk. paper)
1. Women physicians--Fiction. 2. Motherhood--Fiction. I. Bilu, Dalya. II. Title.
PJ5054.C37D6413 2010
892.4'36--dc22
                2010015542

Partially funded by the University of Illinois at Urbana-Champaign
and by a grant from the Illinois Arts Council, a state agency

The Hebrew Literature Series is published in collaboration with
the Institute for the Translation of Hebrew Literature and sponsored by the
Office of Cultural Affairs, Consulate General of Israel in New York

www.dalkeyarchive.com

Cover: design and composition by Danielle Dutton, illustration by Nicholas Motte
Printed on permanent/durable acid-free paper and bound in the United States of America

to my daughter, Osnat

PART ONE

Before goldfish die, they swim for a few hours on their sides, turn over, sink into the shallow water, and float up to the surface again. I once had a little orange goldfish that spent the whole day dying like this, until at dusk it sunk to the bottom of the bowl, its eyes open and its body twisted into a question mark.

I took a plastic cup and fished out the corpse. I went to the kitchen with the cup and poured the water carefully into the sink. I laid the fish on the black marble counter, took a dagger, and began cutting it up. The little shit kept slipping away from me on the counter, so I had to grip it by the tail and return it to the scene of the crime. For about an hour and a half I worked on that fish, until I'd turned its body into little strips you could measure in millimeters.

Then I looked at the pieces. In very ancient times, in the land of Canaan, righteous men would sacrifice bigger animals than this to God. When they cut up a lamb, they would be left with big, bloody, significant pieces in their hands, and their covenant would be a real covenant.

I seasoned the strips of goldfish, put a bit on my finger, lit a match, and brought the flame up to the flesh of the fish until it was a little charred, and my finger too began to smell like a steak. Then I threw my head back, opened my mouth wide, and let the first strip of fish fall straight into my digestive system.

I did the same thing with the rest of the fish, and when I was finished I sat down to contemplate my dying dog, a fourteen-year-old cocker spaniel bitch who was suffering from heart failure. For fifteen days I sat on the armchair and looked at her, at her dry, lolling tongue, her rapid breathing, her dulling eyes. During the course of these fifteen days I gave her food and water, and, of course, medication. She ate and drank next to nothing, and she threw up the medicine. I hooked her up to an IV, into which I injected the drugs, and this helped a little.

I was sorry that I hadn't treated the fish to an IV too, but I immediately dismissed this thought on the grounds that it didn't seem possible to find a vein in such a tiny goldfish. Altogether, it didn't seem possible to find a vein in any fish, even a herring.

After fifteen days of continuous dying, when she no longer ate, stopped drinking, and the medication too became worthless—I allowed myself to open the medicine cabinet and prepared an anesthetic injection from which she'd never wake up.

I went up to her, I stroked her. She licked my fingers with her cleft, sore tongue. She licked my face, her sores scratched my skin, but I didn't mind.

I laid her on my desk, rolling gentle words around on my tongue, murmuring them to her and stroking her orange head while in my other hand was the hypodermic needle.

Even before I'd finished injecting her, my dog closed her eyes and fell asleep. I stroked her and released her neck from the collar bearing all her metal immunization tags, each of them engraved with my address and the promise of a reward for her safe return.

I sat down on my barstool and looked at my fat dog, wondering how long it would take from the moment of the injection for sleep to change into death, and how exactly this changing of the guard took place.

My pet's breathing grew increasingly heavy, deep, and full of significance. Each breath thought itself the last, but another one would always follow to steal away its title. Until . . . It was finished. The dog had had its day.

I called the vet. It was the middle of the night and I woke him up. A few days earlier, when I'd gone to consult him, he'd mumbled something about a man who buried pets for seventy shekels. I asked him for the phone number. He grumbled, "Can't it wait till morning?" and immediately read out the number.

I spoke to the gravedigger and said what I had to say and was just about to hang up when he suddenly broke in:

"I hope you don't think you're coming with me, Miss . . ."

"Excuse me?" I said in astonishment. "Why not? It's my dog you're burying after all. I have every right to be present at the event. What have you got to hide?"

"Listen, lady," he barked, "your seventy shekels is no big deal. Dogs die every other minute. I bury them in the dunes, near the sea. I do it at night, quietly, by myself. Take it or leave it."

The window was wide open, and beyond it, the dark sky was visible, dotted with stars. I was busy working. There was a ring at the door and I cut myself. Blood dripped from three of my fingers. I wrapped them in a little towel and hurried to the door. In front of me stood a short man with a large face and a sagging stomach. He introduced himself by his full name, which immediately evaporated from my mind, and noticed my blood-soaked towel.

"Allow me," he said and came closer.

"No, there's no need," I said. "Really."

But the guest noticed my pallor and shaking knees, led me to the green velvet sofa, and laid me down on it. Then he hurried to the bathroom, took the first-aid kit out of the medicine cabinet, and as he cleaned my wounds with the gentleness of a medical intern, he joked that if he'd come any later, I would have had to pay double, both for the cocker and for myself.

He bandaged my fingers, went into the other room, put the cocker spaniel into a black garbage bag, hoisted it onto his back, and asked for the money in cash. I took the notes out of my pocket. I felt like rolling them up into a tight wad and shoving them horizontally between the gravedigger's upper lip and his nose, like a moustache, but all I did was hand them over and say good-bye, thinking that I would never see him again.

Scarcely a minute had passed, however, before I did—in the distance, from the heights of my thirty-seventh-floor apartment. He tossed the bag with the dog into the trunk and sat down to start the car. But he couldn't get it going, and I thought to myself, here's your chance, Dolly. I ran outside, got into the cylindrical glass elevator, which moved up and down in a series of unnecessary spirals in order to save energy, and made it to the ground floor in time. In a crouched run I made my way across the asphalt, slowly opened the back door, and crawled inside. The little criminal hadn't succeeded in starting the engine yet and was spewing out a sea of curses. It was ten minutes before the charmless solo of the motor was heard, and we set out. I glanced at my watch, it was eight minutes past two, while my compass showed that he was driving west, just as I'd thought.

Twenty minutes later the car signaled a right turn and we drove onto a dirt road full of humps and potholes, on either side of which garish prostitutes displayed themselves. The driver, who apparently had an erection, muttered something to himself, swerved sharply to give one of them a fright, and laughed a wheezing laugh that only subsided some minutes later, when he had turned off the road and receded from the prostitute's view.

The car stopped abruptly and he jumped out with a spade in his hand. I too stole out, into the damp, salty wind blowing from the sea. I hid behind a hillock covered with yellow evening primroses, which didn't remind me of anything, and settled down to watch.

The round pit was dug, and all that remained for this crook to do was drop the bitch into it and cover her up. But instead of finishing his business, he started a whole new ball game. He took the cocker spaniel out of the bag, pulled a pitchfork from the trunk of his car, and began mutilating the corpse, stabbing it, decapitating it, amputating its legs, throwing whatever was left of my dog into the pit and hastily covering it up.

I trembled all over, enraged, a battle cry on my lips. The man turned in surprise and I, in my grief, snatched the pitchfork from his hand, and instead of sticking it into the ground in a civilized manner, I drove it into the gravedigger's stomach with all the strength I'd accumulated over my years of manual labor.

He doubled up in pain. I went berserk and finished him off in a couple of minutes.

Puffing and panting, I stood there for one minute longer. Then I caught my breath, gathered up the pieces of my dog, and buried them in the light of the crescent moon. Finally, I wiped my damp and itchy brow.

I started the car and abandoned myself to a sense of peace I hadn't felt for ages. In this state of serenity I drove that box on wheels back to the main road.

A few seconds after I'd passed the deserted, brightly lit gas station, noticing and not noticing the wavering human silhouette next to the petrol tanks, I began to hear sounds that were incompatible with my surroundings. I couldn't locate these sounds anywhere in the landscape, they seemed to be coming from inside the car itself. I pulled up to the side of the road, and my eyes came to rest on a black plastic bag lying at the back of the car, on the ledge between the backseat and the rear window.

Little cars, mostly Volkswagen Beetles, drove past me in both directions. I waited until the road was momentarily clear, knelt on my seat, and leaned over toward the sound. I opened the plastic bag, and there, wrapped in Health Department diapers, lay a blue, hungry baby.

I rummaged in the bag for documents, looking around for some clues as to the dead man's identity, and in the end, underneath the driver's seat, I found some old income tax forms for a shoe store.

The baby screamed and made sucking motions with his lips. I didn't know what to do to calm him down. I undid the diaper and found a festering hole, two centimeters wide, in the middle of his stomach, surrounded by dried blood. I picked him up and placed him in the passenger seat.

Cars flashed past, all of them Volkswagen Beetles. I threw a glance at my companion. I began to drive, the street lights flickering across his face. The headlights of the cars opposite me dazzled my eyes. I took another peek at the pit in his stomach and remembered coming across the story of a man who'd lived a not inconsiderable number of years ago, and who had agreed, in the interest of medical science, to have a hole left in his stomach, which enabled his physicians to study the functioning of his digestive system. I'd read about this man when I was in my twenties in Katmandu, while I was studying medicine there. I was the only Jew in the university.

I parked the car in the building's underground parking lot. In the cylindrical elevator, which was made of thick, transparent glass, I pressed 37, and within seconds I was in my official residence. It was already morning. I knew that I had to act quickly and efficiently.

I took some anesthetic from one of my cupboards, and consulted my medical books to check the correct amount for anesthetizing a newborn baby. The frogs in the glass aquariums croaked in alarm, thinking I was about to use it on them. I laid the blue, naked baby on my operating table. He screamed. His little mouth gaped like a gondola. I silenced him with the injection, disinfected him, sewed up his stomach, and bandaged the wound. While he was sleeping in the recovery room, hooked up to an IV of drugs and minerals, I walked the streets, and within half an hour I was back in my apartment with everything a baby could need. I prepared a soft, padded room for him, and went out onto the balcony for a cigarette.

I pleaded with myself, I tried building a logical case for postponing the execution for a while, but instead of the voice of reason making itself heard, the situation took control of my eyeballs. They kept looking up, higher and higher, as if there was always something to see up there—more and more sky, a stairway of sky, a Tower of Babel of sky, instead of one deep, blue, unambiguous heaven.

There was no alternative: I injected myself with a sedative that calmed me down, and for the time being the infant's life was spared.

I tried to get my mother on the phone, but the line was busy. When I was a child this woman told me about a mother who'd put her baby in the washing machine and switched it on. The judge sentenced her to life plus hard labor in the prison laundry, as a laundress. So deeply did my mother imprint this story in my mind that even now, while putting the baby's clothes into the washing machine, I imagined seeing the baby in there too, and I fainted.

The baby woke me with his screams, and again—because the influence of the sedative had worn off by now—I wanted to strangle him. But I said to myself: Why waste your energy, Dolly? In any case, that weakling's going to die in a few days' time, of an infection or neglect or carelessness, and even if he does get himself murdered in the end, so what? He should have been dead already anyway.

Nevertheless, my brain started working overtime thinking of a name for the infant. I thought of "Kid." I assumed that he wouldn't survive the age of three. I went on racking my brain for names, but all the while the baby was screaming so hard he nearly burst. I injected an anesthetic into his spine, and he shut up.

I lay down on my giant bed and watched the TV shows picked up by the satellite dishes on the roof, smoking like a chimney as I did so. For a moment I caught myself whistling for the dog, and a string snapped in my body, C sharp, then I closed my eyes, and decided to call him Son, so that if anyone ever called him a son of a bitch, he'd take it personally and beat them up for the both of us.

During the first days of Son's life, I turned thirty, and it was also five years since I had moved into the four hundred story tower. During these years I hadn't made a single friend among my neighbors, except for Itzik, the magician from the forty-seventh floor. When I'd run out of brown sugar or guinea pigs or antidepressants, I would go up to see him.

About a week after I became an unwilling mother, at midnight, I was all ready to go to sleep, but sleep eluded me like a toddler hiding from his parents between the concrete pillars of a parking lot in Ashdod.

There was a heat wave blowing in and it was hot as hell. The air-conditioners weren't working, the lab animals were restless. Only the baby was sleeping—like a corpse.

I realized while still in the elevator that Itzik was throwing a party, no expense spared, no questions asked. Every few weeks this guy would invite all the magicians in town, male and female, to one hell of a party.

The host opened the door. Behind his back appeared the heads of his colleagues, men and women heavily made up.

"*Excusez-moi,*" I simpered, "I wonder if you have a packet full of yellow pills?"

"*Pardonnez-moi,*" said Itzik, "is the shoemaker barefoot?"

"Just say yes or no," I urged him.

"*Pardonnez-moi,*" he said, bowed, and retired into the room, leaving the rectangular space of the door full of dozens of faces examining me with interest. After ten minutes the host reappeared with only twenty pills and a glass of water.

"The stock's finished, Doctor. All I can offer you is an invitation to come in and join us."

He handed me the pills and I swallowed them all on the spot. For almost ten years I've been taking yellow antidepressant pills, which have had no effect on me at all. They were recommended to me by a Thai computer science student I fucked about ten times. I don't know for sure why I go on swallowing more than twenty of these pills a day. I swallow them, they have no taste and no effect either.

In Itzik's living room the magicians were performing that trick where they put some female into a box with three compartments and stick swords into her, and in the end she comes out without a scratch. But this time something went wrong, and terror swept across the magicians like a jet of water from a revolving sprinkler.

"Ai, ai," screamed the model-magician, swords cleaving her body at all kinds of sharp angles without shedding a single drop of blood.

Itzik looked at me, white as an angel. I knew that as a doctor I had to act quickly, but at the same time, as a human being, I didn't really care if the girl died.

"I'm begging you, Dolly, do something." He went down on his knees in a theatrical pose, taking my hand and tenderly kissing my knuckles, which he knew would be hard for me to resist. His lips were dry and cracked from all the forced smiles he smiled at the children's birthday parties, where he put on a double act as a clown and a magician at once.

"I don't know what to tell you," I said. "What's done is done. There was an accident, and the girl died."

"Please, Doctor Dolly. I'm begging you. Take pity on Noga Hasson. She's one of our best. It could happen to anyone."

However much I hated myself for it, when I heard the words "Doctor Dolly"—it gave me a thrill, and Itzik the magician knew it. I went down to my clinic, and a little while later I returned with my bag. All the magicians were sitting on the living room floor playing games that were appropriate to their IQ level. They entered into it wholeheartedly, excited and enthusiastic like a bunch of monkeys.

In the meantime I removed the swords from her body, but far from feeling a sense of dedication and importance, confronting the exalted task of saving a human life, I felt like performing hara-kiri on the patient instead.

After everything was over, the magicians laid the lady on the sofa and licked her wounds, while she kept saying thank you, thank you. At the same time, people came up to me and kissed me on the cheek, and I exchanged a blushing smile with Itzik, who'd fucked me more than twice.

I went home sick of my life and took it out on the bunnies. I tied their ears together, one rabbit's ear to another rabbit's ear, I cut the ears off two other rabbits, one ear each, and sewed them back on the wrong way round.

A thunderstorm began, and heavy clouds, weighing a ton and a half each, collided and inundated Dolly City with blessed rain, flooding roads, filling wells, and shutting mouths.

I went out to the kitchen balcony and lifted the three tiles under which I hid my money. I counted very little and my heart fell. I knew that I didn't have enough money to get through the winter in the style to which I was accustomed. I didn't even have enough to buy firewood.

A piercing chill spread through the house and sank its teeth into my bones. I looked at the snowflakes covering the town with a soft, white blanket. In the grate my last log was burning. I shut the windows, pulled down the blinds, and drew the curtains. I took the polar bear skin I'd once bought in Alaska, which was spread on one of my armchairs, and covered the baby with it. But he was still cold, and in order to forget the chill I began to occupy myself with him. I weighed him, measured the circumference of his head and his length, and entered all this data into the American growth chart. As I sat at my *secretaire*, a book caught my eye. It was a sixteenth-century book on pediatrics, which I'd never opened before. I took it down from the shelf and began to read. It was written in Latin and described horrible childhood diseases, all widespread and fatal at the time. Instead of putting it back and taking down something soothing about dreams, or looking at a Botticelli print, I read on voraciously, and the name of every disease sent a shiver through my heart.

The mite went on sleeping soundly in his cradle, but the information streaming into my brain made my blood run cold. For some reason, I couldn't help associating these diseases with my son. The possibility that he might catch them horrified me, I simply couldn't bear the thought of some disease getting its claws into him. How conscious I was at those moments of the heavy hand of oblivion, which is nothing but infinity in one of its many disguises. I remember I was sucked into some place outside the normal atmosphere. I was terrified, and my terror had a magic, addictive effect. I remember that right at the beginning it was quite exciting. It was like standing a centimeter away from a racing train and feeling the shock waves of that heavy object hurtling through space. I thought to myself, yes, Dolly, fear, the greatest, most terrible fear of them all—it too is merely the shock waves of death.

I found myself lying on the floor, foaming at the mouth. I wiped it and hurried to the bathroom to put my head under ice-cold water. I let the water massage my scalp.

I wrapped my head in a towel, and made up my mind to try to control the terrible fear of losing my child by protecting him as best I could against whatever diseases were out there. I knew that I could never overtake fate, but I decided to try and fight it anyway. I said to myself that the world was full of pitfalls, full of bottomless pits, abysses behind the loquat trees, but that I, as a mother, had to fight against all these troubles, I had to protect this child against countless evil afflictions and natural disasters. I had to keep him safe, keep the lightning and thunder from striking him and the earth from swallowing him up. I declared war to the bitter end: Dolly against the rest of the world. It was as if I said to God that if this child was my responsibility—then he was *my* responsibility. I didn't want favors from anyone, including His Holiness, I didn't want anyone else to do the job for me.

First of all, I decided, I would inoculate the child against as many diseases as possible. I ran outside to buy vaccines against tetanus, whooping cough, diphtheria, polio, measles, jaundice, scarlet fever, small pox, influenza, etc., and I gave them to him all at once—although I knew you shouldn't do this. I couldn't stop myself, I couldn't control my maternal instinct. The child reacted immediately with a high fever and convulsions. It wasn't that it was anything new to me—in the villages of Nepal infants had died in my hands, mothers had torn the bodies of their dead children out of my arms—but this time, with this child, the thought that I might have harmed him sent me into a tailspin of guilt.

I gave him something to bring down his fever, and from forty degrees it plummeted to thirty-four. Hypothermia, the diagnosis echoed grimly inside me. I trembled. The child trembled too and turned blue. I gave him an emergency resuscitation treatment, and after the color began to return to his cheeks, I sat down with him on the rocking chair and rocked for a long time, until he fell asleep.

I put him down in his cot and injected myself with additional sedatives, but to no effect. I lay down on the treatment bed of the domestic hospital I'd set up, and connected myself to the electric current. I gave myself a few jolts to get my head straight.

But I overdid the dosage, and my heart began to fibrillate. I immediately massaged my chest and put an oxygen mask over my face, but nothing helped—I was clinically dead.

Three hours later I opened my eyes. My mother sat opposite me and embroidered. At her feet, on the trampoline, lay the baby. My mother was embroidering a tapestry with a picture of an eighteenth-century woman standing in the middle of a forest and carving the letter S on a tree trunk. My mother was sure that the young woman was carving her lover's name on the tree—but I was sure it was her own name, because she was egocentric as hell.

It was my mother who'd revived me with a special tea she'd brewed according to the specifications of her homeopath. The old woman was firmly opposed to conventional medicine and believed in all other forms of therapy and remedy sneered at by certified physicians. She was convinced that all doctors were murderers, and that it was the doctors who'd killed my father in a sinister conspiracy that also included the cigarette companies and the manufacturers of the hydrochloric acid he'd used to get stains off the bath.

I escorted my mother to the elevator. The transparent door closed behind her, and I watched her sink down through the transparent floors. I ran to the balcony and managed to catch sight of her crossing the street.

"Mother," I screamed, "Mother, Mother—" The trains rushed past at the speed of a typhoon.

I ordered from abroad the most up-to-date medical encyclopedia about children's diseases and their treatment. For days on end I devoured all the names and descriptions and learned them by heart. This was a terrible mistake, because the up-to-date information was far more complex than I'd imagined, and when at last I understood it, it felt like some sort of sex maniac had been let loose inside me, wreaking havoc.

Frantic, I rushed to my laboratory. I looked at all the cages, at the animals and their bleary eyes, at the centrifuges, the bottles, the test-tubes, the cupboard where I kept solutions with billions of germs of dangerous diseases, supposed by many to be extinct, but which I had succeeded in my experiments to revive and coax into resisting common vaccines.

I shuddered. My hair stood on end, the heavy curtains on the windows soared, the copy machine duplicated the same document a thousand times without any command on my part. The X-ray machine shot sparks and crackled.

The animals saw me shivering and scurried round their cages in panic. They knew what I knew—that I had to prevent my son from being infected by these diseases at all costs. I poured disinfectant over my hands and scrubbed them for half an hour, until my skin puckered and began to peel and my fingerprints were almost rubbed out. Then I filled a bathtub with an antiseptic solution and sat in it for an hour and a half considering what to do with the laboratory. Should I set it on fire? Should I employ a lab assistant to operate it and give her instructions from a safe distance? Or perhaps I should lock it up, and let nature take its course.

While I sat trembling and twitching between these alternatives, the terrible fear of my son's possible premature demise continued to mount, until I found myself standing over him and watching him breathe, for fear that he might suddenly be snatched from me by crib death. The names of diseases were no longer simply names, but menacing, dangerous entities in and of themselves. I'd inflated these disasters to mythological proportions, and it was driving me out of my mind.

A voice kept calling out inside me: Destroy the laboratory, bury your sinister career for the sake of the infant's bright tomorrows. Burn it down, for the sake of the next generation.

I locked the laboratory and barred the door so that no disease lurking in the depths of some test-tube would escape and get its claws into my son. As a doctor I knew that the only remedy against disease was to stay healthy.

All that night I stopped myself from breaking into the lab and trying something new. I touched the black wooden door, behind which swarmed the life over which I exerted my control: mice running round little cages, rabbits pink and sick with ten diseases at once, suffering the torments of hell and wishing they were dead. In another minute I was going to break in and drown myself in these diseases of my own creation. In my terror I rushed to the baby's room. I ripped off the blankets and saw the little head, the tiny body. I strained my eyes—could it be possible? The child had stopped breathing! I ran to fetch the stethoscope, and put the cold metal disk on the place where the little heart was situated. My ears filled with rapid heartbeats, and I was relieved.

I changed his diaper, and as the child lay naked on his back I suddenly realized that I never had him circumcised. Right away I opened the phone directory and looked for a mohel to perform the ceremony. Since I had no recommendations, I chose a name at random.

I dialed the number, and while I waited I tried to imagine what a mohel's voice sounds like. I imagined that it would probably be hoarse due to wear-and-tear, and indeed the man was very hoarse. As a matter of fact, when we met at the intersection of two streets undermining each other, he asked me to do him a favor and push him under a moving train instead of paying him for the job.

He told me that he had cancer of the vocal cords, and that he couldn't afford to lose his voice. All his life he'd wanted to be a cantor in a synagogue but his voice wasn't good enough. His brother's was, and he was a famous cantor. I stole a glance at the mohel's face, purple in the neon light, and got myself out of there.

I came home and burst into Son's room. I whipped out my stethoscope and checked to see if he was alive. He was alive, and he even looked at me with a hint of reproach in his eyes. But I couldn't control myself. I wanted to give him a blood test. He seemed pale, as if he had a vitamin B12 deficiency.

I rushed like a woman possessed to my clinic, next to the lab. I turned the key and went in to get sterile instruments. I cut the child in his foot and took blood. And then I panicked again, fearing I had lost him, and I checked his heart again. His heartbeat was normal, but I panicked. I thought I heard a murmur.

I wanted to perform open-heart surgery on him. I ran to the operating room and started getting it ready. While I was sterilizing the knives, I remembered that I'd left the baby with an open wound, and he must be losing a lot of blood. I burst into the room and saw my son fading away as his blood dripped to the floor.

Blood, blood, I needed a blood donation. But where was I going to get a blood donation from? I wasn't the blood bank, and I didn't have their phone number either. The few people I'd operated on in my life had all died on the operating table. My career was a living example of the rule: the operation was a success but the patient died. The little mite's sheet was completely red by now. Yes, the incision I had made was too deep. I ran back to the clinic, took out my sewing kit and closed him up with butterfly strips. I examined his heart. The beat was even and distant, like war drums at the other end of the world.

I'm losing him—the thought echoed hollowly inside me, and once more I was filled with fear. But I got hold of myself. I became professional. I cut a vein in my arm, inserted a tube, and prayed that it would work.

When I opened my eyes, my life gained a new dimension. The color had come back to my baby's cheeks, the blinds were open, my mother was sitting in the rocking chair and embroidering, and two cabbage butterflies were fluttering about the room.

The baby's cot was clean, everything was white and fresh.

"How long have you been sitting here?" I asked, still dazed.

"A few minutes, only a few minutes." She fell silent. I raised myself slightly and leaned on my elbows.

"Tell me, Dolly," she began. "Why don't you throw out those disgusting mice of yours? Why are your knives dirty? Why are your hypodermic needles rusty? What are you trying to prove—that there's no God?" She fixed me with her beady little eyes.

"I'm trying to find a cure for cancer," I said after a long pause.

"Don't mock me," she said. "This isn't the way you look for a cure for cancer. This is the way you get up to monkey business. You only cut for the sake of cutting."

"That's not true," I defended myself.

"And why didn't you invite me to the baby's bris?" she asked after a moment.

"What bris?" I ripped the diaper from my baby's loins and realized—she was right.

"You're getting senile, aren't you?" she said and pointed to the four photo albums lying at the end of the room. I leafed through one of them, it was incredible: the standard pictures of a bris in a big hall, with a band and refreshments. There were a lot of people there, but it was impossible to distinguish them from each other.

"There's a video cassette too," she said and pointed to the snowy television screen.

I went through all the albums and watched the video over and over again, but I was unable to make out a single face. Naturally I couldn't see the mohel either. The only one to come out clearly on the video was my sister, who was tangoing on the dance floor. I called her up to ask who the mohel was, and she gave me the phone number of the national airline, Pan-T, baggage department.

When I phoned Pan-T, I had a déjà vu. My father had worked for Pan-T for thirty-two years before he died.

In the baggage department they told me that they did indeed have a mohel working there, and they put him on the line. The mohel was discreet; he refused to tell me who had hired him, revealing only that it was a tall, sturdy man with silver hair, and as far as he knew, a senior pilot with the airline. He thought he was the baby's grandfather. I asked for more details about the child's potential grandfather, but the man told me no more.

I gave my mother a sleeping pill, and she fell off the chair and lay snoring on the carpet. I fed the baby, nurtured him with some anti-infection medicines, and put him to sleep. I took two pistols from my armory, one for my right hand and one for my left, together with a few other gadgets, and went out.

It was August, snow was falling softly. It covered all the roads and pavements, and people were walking about wearing Russian fur hats. I stopped a cab and asked the driver to take me to Ben Gurion Airport. At Ben Gurion it was summer, the sun beat down on the cosmopolitan heads with calm tyranny. I went into the public lavatories and peeled off a few layers of clothing. I put them into a suitcase and sent them home.

Resolutely I strode into my late father's office, the company's salaries department. I knew they had an up-to-date list of the pilots' names.

I whipped out one of my pistols and shouted at the secretary:

"The pilots' names, and be quick about it!"

"But it's confidential, Dolly," she said, and I stuck a bullet in her heart.

A dwarfish clerk advanced slowly towards a filing cabinet, murmuring that he was crazy about Luis Buñuel. I gave him one between the ribs. The new head of the department, who'd taken my father's place, was shaving underneath the table. I let him have it. Nothing personal.

I opened the filing cabinets. Everything was still organized the same way. I recognized my father's handwriting on a few of the labels. I found the list of pilots without any problem—all I had to do was look for the names with the biggest salaries—and strode rapidly out of the shed where my father had killed himself.

I entered the boss's office and injected Ashkenazi\Idelman\Mimelman with galloping syphilis on the grounds that he'd intimidated and humiliated my father. He begged me to cure him, and I pretended to consider it and promised to give him a massage, and so got him to come home with me.

As soon as I walked into the flat with my prisoner I gave him a shot in the ass, laid him down on a stretcher, tied him down, and suspended a string from the ceiling with a hungry, demented rat hanging at the end of it. I didn't know which of them I was torturing more, but it gave me a thrill anyway.

Then I had another severe attack, and instead of taking it out on the bare chest of the prisoner, I took it out on my baby. Again the two words "heart murmur" surfaced in my mind, like a rustle heard in the undergrowth during an ambush, and I froze where I stood, like a hypnotized person when she hears someone say the magic trigger words that have been implanted in her mind. I remembered that in the heat of my revenge, I'd forgotten to examine the little one's heart.

I appeared in his room with the lethal tray. I tied the green surgeon's mask around my face and began giving him every test in the book. Everything was fine, the kid was okay, he had a fine heart, not a murmur to be heard. But even though the child was a hundred percent healthy, I decided to cut him open. I succumbed to the chronic doubt from which I suffer. I wanted to check and see with my own eyes that everything was really in order, and then to check up on my checkup, and then to make sure that there hadn't been any slipups in the re-examination, and so on and so forth.

I gave the child anesthetic, I put him to sleep, and I did it. I slipped my hands into white gloves and began slicing into his thorax. His internal organs were revealed to my searching gaze, his heart, his lungs. Once I'd opened him up, I poked around in there too. Then I opened up his stomach, I held an organ roll call, I demanded to know if they were all present and correct.

Everything was in place, there were no deviations from the norm. I confirmed this again and again, I repeated my examination tirelessly, I opened books and compared notes—everything was one hundred percent okay.

All this went on for about six hours. I closed him up and gave him a blood transfusion to revive him. I was reassured. I sat in the armchair, let my head fall back, and looked at the second hand of the clock on the wall. In the interrogation room my father's employer screamed and whimpered. Because of him it took me more than an hour to hear my little lamb bleating, and I hurried to his room.

I looked at the huge scar running all the way down his body. Instead of being sorry that he wouldn't be able to wear bikini briefs—I was consumed by doubts, I disappeared into them like Saint-Exupéry disappeared into the sky. I was overwhelmed with regret for not having operated on his head while I was at it. I wiped this thought clear out of my mind, and went to change the prisoner's rat. The hero didn't blink an eye, even though his face was already torn to shreds.

There was an unspoken agreement between us that he deserved it.

I took the list of pilots and a can of Diet Coke and went out to the balcony. Under the open sky everything looks clearer. I marked the names of the pilots who seemed tall and silver-haired with a fluorescent marker. I dialed the number of one of the silver princes of the air and his wife answered.

"Hello," I said, "can I speak to Armand Levy?"

"Who wants him?"

"Dolly. Doctor Dolly. I'm speaking from Pakistan and I haven't got any time to waste. Please hurry!"

"Sorry, Armand's not at home. He's on a flight."

"When will he be back?"

"Tomorrow at eight."

The baby screamed. I hung up. The boss had fainted. I pulled up the string with the rat, and smeared his open wounds with rabbit droppings. Immediately after that I picked up my son and rocked him to and fro to calm him down.

I sung him various songs as we approached the balcony railing. Sometimes, even in Dolly City, I feel like a stranger. I look at the traffic jams, I listen to the ding-dong of the big clock tower, the gong of the Chinese restaurant, but in spite of it all I begin to tremble, I want to go home—even though this is my home.

I looked down at the trash heaps, the carcasses, the distant ships, and I felt dizzy. For a moment I was close to tossing the baby out. Ten times over I rechecked that I was still holding him, moving back before I did something I'd be sorry for later. It was the same lousy trap. The mere fact that it was theoretically possible for me to throw him off the balcony was enough to give me the heebie-jeebies—as if I'd already done it.

I called a welder and ordered bars. I said to myself, with children it's no joke, you don't take risks.

An hour later there was a ring at the door. The welder and I went from room to room, balcony to balcony, window to window. I even asked him to bar the holes in the bath and the basin. I don't want any trouble, I told him, you might as well put little bars on the taps too.

"Lady," he finally said, "are you completely crazy?"

"I only want to be sure," I said.

"I won't be a part of this lunacy, sorry." He turned to go.

"What do you care?" I called after him. "I'm paying you aren't I?"

He turned round, and with the same movement he flung his ruler to the far end of the room.

"Pick that up," I said authoritatively. "I don't have to put up with your tantrums."

"My tantrums? Mine?" he yelled and turned completely red. "My tantrums, you say? Mine?" And he stiffened for a moment and then fell senseless to the floor, and there was nothing left for me to do but confirm his death, pick him up, and throw him down to the hungry Arab workers living on the first floors of the building—let them eat him if they liked. In the same manner I got rid of my prisoner, of whom there was hardly anything left.

I called another welder who didn't ask any questions. By midnight the whole house was barred. I stood on the balcony and breathed. The air was still, and the tops of the soft towers, which usually swayed in the wind, were stiff and erect as masts. The bars were ruining the view, without which my life wasn't worth living. Shivers ran down my spine, my forehead was as cold as steel. I made up my mind that first thing in the morning I'd call in a welder to get rid of all these bars. They were driving me crazy, and if I was afraid that in a moment of stupefaction I might toss the child out of the window—well there were only two possibilities, either I would or I wouldn't. The fact that there were only two options available, and that the possibilities weren't endless, gave me a brief feeling of confidence. Confidence in what, I don't know.

In the morning a welder arrived and took the bars down. After he piled them up on the living room floor he said: "What do you want me to do with them, Miss?"

"As far as I'm concerned you can swallow them, shithead," I said, upset. The welder stared at me in astonishment.

"Excuse me, Miss, but there's no need to be so agitated."

"Don't tell me what to do, asshole! And get your ugly mug out of here."

He gave me a friendly smile, hoisted a few of the crooked bars onto his back, and turned to go.

"There's a letter for you under the door," he called, bent down, and handed me an envelope. It was letter number one thousand and something in the correspondence I'd been conducting for the past three years with the bureaucrats and functionaries about their refusal to approve my medical degree from Katmandu, and their insistence that I undergo lengthy additional training in Beersheba, which I refused to do. I have no intention of taking any more courses, ever. Eight years in the University of Katmandu were quite enough for me.

When I bought this apartment, the previous occupant told me that it had been designed by a Bedouin architect, who had lived in it years before and who'd possessed a tremendous sense of space. I don't know the exact measurements in meters, maybe it's a more like a kilometer, but it's three hundred square meters at least.

From time to time various pieces of furniture would fly out of the skyscraper windows, and sometimes my line of longitude would be crossed by suicides whose screams were swallowed up in the terrific noise of the trains and cars and airplanes.

I sat on the balcony and looked outside. The flies were bothering my baby. I slowly sipped my decaffeinated coffee with cyclamate-free sugar and turned on a fan to chase away the flies. Once again, terrible thoughts began to emerge from the depths of my despair and crush me like pythons. I tried to fight them by letting them express themselves and letting them go as far as they would, and indeed, when I confronted the worst and looked disaster in the eye, I felt somewhat calmer.

From the minute the Pan-T airline came into my life again I felt a certain relief, and so, I assume, did the child, since instead of harassing him and upsetting my peace of mind, I began harassing the airline pilots. I developed the fear that one fine day one of them would come and take my little project away from me, claiming that he was his grandfather. I couldn't bear the thought of any other Pan-T employee touching my son, let alone feeling he had grandfatherly rights to him.

I played a tune from a music box to the child, the same tune about two hundred and fifty times, until he vomited the goat's milk he'd just gobbled up all over himself, and I began harassing the pilots to increasing degrees, just like burns. I began with the first degree. I ordered Dutch cheeses and pizzas with onion rings to be delivered to their addresses. I lay in wait for their children when they came out of school, and filled their mandolins with shit, I flooded the pilots with telegrams consoling them on the death of a loved one, and I sent them countless press clippings about planes that had crashed or that disappeared over the Bermuda Triangle.

I only wanted to upset their self-confidence a little, shake the Persian carpet under their feet. I wanted to prove to them that you can drown in fire, get burnt by water, and not just theoretically either.

One night I woke up at three o'clock in the morning with an intense desire to operate. Once upon a time, when the urge took me, I would find myself in my laboratory, opening and closing animals, but now that my research was shelved and the lab was taboo there was nothing for me to do, and in any case there was nothing left for me to operate on, since dissecting dead bodies bored me stiff.

At the bottom of my heart I knew I must not, I definitely must not go into the baby's room. He was sleeping soundly. I advanced on him wearing my green surgeon's uniform, undressed him, and laid him on his belly on the cold metal table. He shivered with cold. I counted his vertebrae. It seemed to me that there was one missing. I counted them again and again, and after I was one hundred percent, two hundred percent—and so on in arithmetic progression up to a million percent—certain, I started feeding all kinds of data on my child into the computer, until it began to groan like a woman in labor.

The baby was still lying on his stomach. I put him to sleep, even though I still didn't know where I was going to cut. I tried desperately to suppress this drive of mine to mess with the child, I tried pacifying it with a simple enema, but to no avail.

I took a knife and began cutting here and there. I drew a map of the Land of Israel during the Biblical period on his back, just as I remembered it from school, and marked in all those Philistine towns like Gath and Ashkelon, and with the blade of the knife I etched the Sea of Galilee and the Jordan River, which empties out into the Dead Sea that goes on evaporating nonstop.

Drops of blood began welling up in the river beds cutting across the country. The sight of the map of the Land of Israel, amateurishly sketched on my son's back, gave me a shiver of delight. At long last I felt that I was cutting into living flesh. My baby screamed in pain—but I stood firm. When I'd finished marking all the sites my neglected education succeeded in pulling out of the creaking drawers of my mind, I went back to being what I am—a doctor—and I disinfected and dressed the cuts, and sewed them up where necessary.

I contemplated his carved-up back: it was the map of the Land of Israel, nobody could mistake it.

At night, when I couldn't sleep, I would go out to the balcony and try to pull myself together. Dolly City lay below me in all its chaos and ugliness. Dolly City, a fragmented city, a crosshatched city, one motherfucking city.

I tried to ignore the terrible noise of the metropolis, the clatter of the machines, the screeching and rattling of the traffic, which behaved as if Dolly City belonged to it. Cable cars, steam engines, express trains, ships, trams, airplanes, automobiles, trucks, motorbikes—they all crossed each other's routes, colliding with each other, freaking me out, making me frantic.

In the middle of the day the sky was one big traffic jam of leaden planes. I would search for a bit of blue sky and fix my eyes on it. These were rare moments when I would try with all my might and main to feel part of a world far wider than Dolly City, but it was almost impossible. I was my own prisoner. I couldn't escape. All I could do was look at the jet-propelled trains being swallowed up in the black tunnels of infinity, of other people, of the rest of the world.

One evening I lay on the carpet and surveyed my son's body meticulously, as if he was right next to me, instead of in the next room. The computer located trouble spots in the lower back region, and a thought reared up inside me: the kidneys, Dolly. You didn't examine his kidneys! I forcefully restrained myself from moving. With a thousand tongues I persuaded my cracked and peeling hands not to touch the baby, to be content with routine tests in order to check if the kidneys were functioning properly.

The whole of the next day I pored over his urine, trying to discover worrying signs of albumin, or clear traces of an infection, but the child was healthy. This had never bothered me in the past, and it didn't bother me now either. I opened him up. I dug and delved, I poked and prodded and stared and paled: the child had one kidney. I counted fifty times over, and "one" was the result that came up most often.

I sunk into depression. It was a foregone conclusion: a transplant was unavoidable. I racked my brains as to where the hell I was going to find a kidney, and in the end I came up with a five-year plan.

I took a taxi to Ben Yehuda Street, to the Pan-T building. I walked into the building with measured steps, and sat down opposite a diligent clerk who was busy making calculations. She muttered the figures and arithmetic operations aloud to herself, as if she were praying.

I waited for five minutes until she looked at me inquiringly.

"Yes," I said to her. "That's right. Look at me, go on, look."

"That's what I'm doing isn't it?" she said and turned red. "That's what I've been doing for fifteen years, isn't it?" She stood up, utterly overwrought.

"Calm down," I said. "Take a deep breath, and don't be so sensitive. Let go."

"You think it's easy?" she barked rudely. "You . . ."

"Look at me," I interrupted her. "Do I look familiar to you?"

"No."

"Look harder, you slut. These features. The nose. Pay attention to the nose. Especially the lower part. The nostrils. The small eyes. The pale eyebrows. The nervousness, the nerves. How many more hints do you need?"

"The more the merrier."

"My father was an employee of your company."

"I'm delighted to hear it."

"His name was S—"

"Who cares?"

"He was the head of the salaries department. He died of mesothelioma. An extremely rare form of lung cancer. You get it from asbestos. In the medical literature, only . . ."

"Stop right there!" cried the clerk in alarm. "No talk of illnesses, please. I'm a hypochondriac."

"And I'm a doctor."

"Seriously?" Her eyes lit up for a moment, but were immediately clouded by insanity as she leaned forward and whispered, "Look at my eyes, honey, give me an off-the-cuff diagnosis. Are the pupils the same?"

"Yes."

"Thank God," she said in relief, and her eyes were clear again, but the next minute they darkened, as she pointed to a light brown spot on the back of her hand, "And this mark, is it cancer?"

"I don't think it's cancer."

"Do me a favor. My brother suffers from migraines. Could it be the beginning of meningitis? How long does it take before you know if you've been infected as well?"

"Give me a ticket to Düsseldorf, business class, and I want a discount."

"Why?"

"Because you've got cancer. You're going to die. You have to fight it. You must never give in!" I clenched my fist and waved it in the air.

"I have to fly," she grabbed her purse and hastily straightened the knot in her brightly colored scarf.

"Where do you think you're going?" called the girl sitting next to her. But the diligent clerk took no notice and rushed straight into the street.

"Actually, I need two tickets," I said to the second clerk. "One for me and one for my baby. How much will I get off if my father worked for Pan-T in the years . . ."

"Nothing. Your right to a discount or a free ticket died with him."

She made all kinds of calculations and in the end she threw a sum at me and I wrote a postdated check. When I stepped outside, the two tickets in my hand, I looked at the spiraling steps climbing up the outside of the Pan-T building. I reached the roof and was just about to take one hell of an Olympic dive, but at the last minute I saw a Pan-T plane making its way in the direction of the blue sea, and I watched it until it vanished into the white clouds.

It took me three days to sterilize all my operating instruments and pack them up, and the very next day I was fastening my seat belt and that of my son, and we flew away into the unknown. Sitting next to me was a tank who must have weighed at least two hundred kilos, with swarthy skin and a wig on his head. He was suffering from a toothache and he was crying, and the flight attendants came and went with painkillers and glasses of cognac to put the area to sleep. Nothing helped, except for the sedative I injected into the lower regions of his paunch, which silenced him, apparently for good. I wanted to use the opportunity to have a nap, but suddenly I saw a flight attendant running up the aisle and crying in all directions:

"Is there a doctor on the plane? Is there a doctor on the pl—"
Nobody got off their ass but me.

I said, "I'm a doctor, what's the problem?"

"Come with me," she said and tore the baby from his seat. "There's a woman about to give birth."

"Where is she?"

"In the pilot's cabin."

"And who's the pilot?"

"Goldberg."

"Aha." As far as I remembered, there was no Goldberg on the list.

"Is he new?"

"Old as the hills. On his way out. His daughter went to school with me. She doesn't even look Jewish," she looked at the little golden Magen David nestling on my chest, "she's so pretty. She's studying medicine at the Technion."

"Medicine at the Technion?" I said in amazement. "You can't study medicine at the Technion."

"No?" the flight attendant shrugged.

I helped some woman lying on the floor of the pilot's cabin to give birth. It turned out to be a boy, dead. I sewed her up, waiting all the time for the pilot to turn round, so I could see if there was any resemblance between him and my son, but he kept his eyes in front of him all the time.

The decision to fly with the child to Düsseldorf, Germany, in order to obtain a kidney for him from a German baby, was made on purely moral grounds. At first I thought in practical terms. Where, I thought, could I kidnap a baby and remove his kidney, without caring? The first place that leapt to mind was Brazil, where one-year-olds already run brothels. But Brazil sounded too far away, and who's got the energy to dance the samba? Then I thought: an Arab baby. They hate us, we hate them. I'll kidnap an Arab baby, remove his kidney, and transplant it in the body of my only son. But then I frowned. Everyone knows that you can't mess with Arabs, even talking to them is dangerous, and if you turn your back on them you're dead. And then I sat and thought about the history of mankind. Who of all the people that ever lived were the biggest pigs, which of them had broken all the records? The answer was clear.

It was no skin off my nose to take some German baby from an orphanage in Düsseldorf, cut out his kidney, and donate it to my son. On the contrary, I even felt a sense of vocation. I knew I was doing the right thing. Worst-case scenario, I might end up killing a German baby or two.

Already on the way to the hotel, in a taxi following the minibus containing the Israeli Pan-T aircrew, we passed a gang of neo-Nazis carrying posters in their language and waving their fists at the Jewish minibus.

The hotel was incredible. I'd never in my life seen such wealth and splendor. The waiters were well-scrubbed, the reception clerk was smooth as a baby's bottom, and he gave me the keys to my room on the hundred and seventy-third floor.

As soon as I entered my suite, I took care of the baby for a bit until he fell asleep, and then I leafed through the German phone directory. I was looking for orphanages off the beaten track, abandoned institutions in forest clearings, cellars in godforsaken villages. I found a few.

I packed the child in a perforated suitcase and went out into the pouring rain to hunt for a taxi.

The rain beat down on my thick skull, beat down on the suitcase, got in through the holes and wet the baby, who sneezed nonstop. I cursed myself for not bringing my X-ray machine along, I would have taken an X-ray of his lungs right there and then to see if he was developing something.

The taxi driver was a typical German schmuck. A loathsome creature who made me want to puke right on him, a real subhuman. He criticized the way I was keeping my baby. I didn't even answer him. The day some German tells me what to do and I take any notice of him—that'll be the day chickens grow teeth.

The imbecile went on passing remarks but I controlled myself. He's my child, and I'm entitled to bring him up the way I see fit. I wanted to teach him something nobody ever taught me—to live in the privacy of his own four walls.

We entered the forest, and it began to snow. After driving for about thirty minutes on muddy paths, I let the driver go next to a lonely, dilapidated old house, and I knocked on the rusty iron door.

I was tense and out of breath. I just wanted to get it over with and go back home to Dolly City. I'm not cut out for world travel. The door was opened by a young brunette, who announced that her name was Stephanie Poldark, and that she was a nymphomaniac. But what did it matter.

It wouldn't have taken a genius to guess that Stephanie Poldark was a bullshit name. She brought out a fantastic cheesecake with whipped cream and decorations, it was really something. After I had polished off three slices—those yellow antidepressants give you a craving for sweets—I asked her in English if her grandfather on her mother's side was an officer in the S.S.

"No," she replied. "My grandfather on my *father's* side was an officer in the S.S. I'm so ashamed of it, you can't imagine! That's the reason I decided to devote my life to helping others," she said and embraced three of her little wards, who clustered for shelter under her wings. But their kidneys were of no interest to me. I was looking for someone of Son's age.

"I want to entrust this baby to your devoted care," I said and took him out of the suitcase. "He's yours. I don't fancy him any more."

"Hand him over," she said. "He's Jewish, isn't he? It's so obvious!" She stroked him tenderly and kissed his fingers—something I'd never even come close to doing.

"But first of all," I said, "I want to stay here for a few days, to check the place out . . ."

"Yes . . ." said Stephanie Poldark, but it was obvious that she was deep in thought. "Sometimes I ask myself," she said, from a dense cloud of contemplation, "how long? How long will I go on devoting my life to others? When will I, at last, be able to start fucking whoever I feel like fucking? How long do I have to go on serving this sentence I passed on myself? I want to be free! Free of this guilt! I can't take it any more." She fell silent and her tears dripped onto my baby's face.

"Stephanie Poldark," I said suddenly, because I knew that an open wound was a great doorway to opportunity, "I want free access to the kidneys of all your babies up to the age of six months."

"Whatever you like," she said. "Just do me one favor. If you're already opening them up—open their heads too. See if there's a screw loose somewhere in our German heads."

I said sure, but I had no intention whatsoever to actually check. What good would it do to know that German heads are full of shit?

I worked all night long. I tried all the kidneys of all the forty babies of the proper age in the orphanage. Some of them died on me. I left them lying there with their guts spilling out, and took a coffee break.

At five in the morning I transplanted Sonny's new kidney. I sewed him up, and with the string I had left over I stuck a few butterfly stitches onto the rest of the surviving babies, but the butterflies, instead of staying where they were and stopping the flow of blood, flew right out and the babies expired one after the other.

I felt a bit uncomfortable when I saw Stephanie Poldark, who'd been such a charming hostess. I didn't know how to tell her that a few dozen babies had kicked the bucket. But she took it in stride, and said dryly that there was no need for me to feel any guilt whatsoever.

The transplant was a success, the organ was accepted by the body, and everything went according to plan.

I said good-bye to Stephanie and her children and flew back home. On the return flight, too, the flight attendant asked if there was a doctor on the plane, and some woman called Judy stood up. If she's a doctor, I said to myself, then I'm Dr. Zhivago. But I kept quiet. People who live in glass houses shouldn't throw stones.

Five minutes after I walked through the door I felt a new attack coming. The gnawing doubts, the fear and the trembling. And what, I asked myself, what if the baby never had a kidney missing in the first place? What if I'd been mistaken, and my son now had three kidneys? I'm only human after all—I'd almost certainly made a mistake.

If anyone had made a mistake it was more likely to be me than God.

That cloud, that familiar, wretched black cloud, entered my soul and filled it with soot. Operate! I said to myself. Operate! Check it out! Make sure!

A thousand times, I counted. Once I counted two, and once three. Once I came up with four, and another time—with one. I could have taken him to be examined by a normal doctor, but I didn't trust anybody, and of course, I didn't want to expose myself either. So, what was I to believe? How many kidneys did he have? How many kidneys did my baby have? I decided to give it a rest and come back after a break.

I gave him an anesthetic shot and left him open on the bureau, like a telephone off the hook, while I lay down on the carpet. I couldn't fall asleep. In the end I went and knocked on the door of my neighbor, Itzik, who was in the middle of mauling some woman's clit, and I said:

"Do me a favor, I need a second opinion. I don't feel so good. Can you come and count my baby's kidneys?"

"You've got a baby?" he asked in astonishment. "Whose is it?"

"What do you mean whose is it?" I snapped and changed the subject. "What a mess, what a mess. You have no idea how bad." We went into the elevator.

"Tell me," he said, "how am I supposed to know if it's the kidneys? How do I know it's not the liver?"

"All you have to do is count—I'll tell you what you're counting," I said dryly.

Itzik the magician counted three kidneys, and I fainted. He thought I was dead and was about to throw me out of the window, but fortunately I opened my eyes just in time. I sent him on his way, and hurried back to poke inside my child. He began to lose blood, and I, fool that I am, forgot which was the transplanted kidney. I couldn't tell it from the originals. In the end I took a shot in the dark, chose one of them at random, and ripped it out. If this child was fated to die on the operating table—what could I do about it? I was doing everything humanly possible to save him.

I closed him up with a patch of skin I sliced off my thigh, and lay down on the carpet to read the Dolly City news, but I couldn't concentrate. I felt as heavy as an IDF tank, together with a strong desire for radical change. I longed to get away from Dolly City, to abandon it, to banish it from my sight as if it was a mangy mutt dogging my steps. Dolly City was driving me crazy. I was so desperate I even stopped harassing the pilots.

I looked out of the window, but how long can you go on looking out of the window at rushing trains? Especially when they're rushing to where these trains were rushing. All the trains in Dolly City rushed to Dachau and back again. Not *that* Dachau, just some old plank with the name Dachau written on it, a kind of memorial. How long can you let your eyes work overtime, flipping through images until you can't see straight anymore?

There had to be a solution.

June, July, August, September, were already behind me. The child was already nine months old, and the danger of him suddenly dying of crib death had decreased. I went on giving him routine examinations and occasional cosmetic surgeries to smooth out the scars. I had an idea—more like an invention, really—instead of opening and closing a person up every time you had to look inside him, you could install a kind of little Venetian blind in the weak spot, and then all you'd have to do would be to roll up the slats and peep through them.

The day the child turned one and stood up on his hind legs and began to walk, and I saw before me a person, small, but a person nevertheless—I got the idea into my head that maybe he was developing cancer. The fear of cancer was the worst of all. Cancer, in my opinion, is the most important disease that the Angel of Death has invented to date. This disease is one big trap, both for the doctor and for the patient, because you can never know with absolute certainty if it has already begun to bloom in the depths of a person's body. Nipping it in the bud is like trying to catch a bird by jumping into the sky. Even if you catch it in midair you fall flat on your face and break your jaw, if you're lucky.

Throughout my research in bygone days I'd tried with all my might to find a cure for this disease—but it was not to be. During my experiments I would always stray to other fields. The wings of imagination carried me beyond cancer, to research for research's sake, and thus I found myself carving up all kinds of animals just for the hell of it.

And so, although he didn't have cancer, he didn't have cancer, although he definitely didn't have cancer, I still decided to give him a course of chemotherapy and large amounts of vitamin A.

Just to be on the safe side.

The child grew thin, his hair fell out, but I knew: this dreadful disease had to be fought, it had to be stopped.

I didn't sleep at night. First of all, the trains and the expressway drove me crazy. Over the years, the population of Dolly City grew and it filled up with all kinds of nonentities and subhumans, who demanded more and more means of transport, more and more roads and railways. For lack of space, new roads and railways were built one on top of the other, and the terrible noise of the trains became such an integral part of my being that sometimes I thought it was a figment of my imagination.

And yet every time I thought so, I got up to make sure. To make sure again. And again, and again. Until I was absolutely, absolutely, absolutely certain that the trains I saw down below, the colliding cars, the commotion of the modern world, were really and truly there. The echo took over my life to such an extent that I was unable to distinguish it from the original sound.

These symptoms of my disease, the disease of infinite possibilities, the determination of doubt, would even manifest themselves in relation to the very existence of my child. Sometimes, in particularly difficult moments, I would send an SOS to my mother to come and tell me what I saw, on the basis of her experience. She would say: That's a table, Dolly, that's a chair, this is a living room, this is an open-circuit television. I'm your mother, you're Dolly, and here's a baby. What a beautiful baby! What a darling baby!

What a regression! What a catastrophe! At the age of thirty-something, the old woman had to come and prove to me that the ball was round, the ball was red, the ball was green and bouncing.

The one who really benefited from all these superfluous explanations was the precious child. He would listen to my mother with his big, black eyes wide open. His head was so small, like a tennis ball, that sometimes I felt like giving it a bash and serving it over the net.

Before going any further, I would like to stress something: I don't want to give the impression here that I took a child and destroyed him. I only wanted to protect him from harm. I wanted him to live to a hundred and twenty, and what's wrong with that? I wanted to be in command on all fronts, and what's wrong with that? Why this hypocrisy? In some societies a man can be forced to chop off his sister's clitoris with his teeth—and I'm not entitled to demand sovereignty over the defense of my son?

PART TWO

Winds blew, evil winds, winds that pissed on the citizens, piss disguised as rain. I looked out at the ceaseless movement of this city, at the frenzy of the traffic, at the fury of the buses forced to wait for all the lost, senile old ladies to get on, at the conductors who spent their breaks fucking the drivers on the moldy backseats. My house stank too, it exuded the smell of ancient dampness.

According to my calculations, Son was now one year and ten months old. He sat on the carpet and played with all the sterile toys I made him—pasteurized carcasses of lab animals, sterilized frogs. He put them in his mouth and chewed and chewed, like a cow, getting on my nerves and preventing me from watching *McMillan & Wife* on TV.

It drove me up the wall, this sound of tireless chewing, and until I locked him in the closet, I couldn't watch McMillan going down on his wife in peace.

I settled down on the sofa again to watch the copulating couple. For five consecutive episodes they'd been showing the same serialized screw. You really have to hand it to them, the way they drag it out.

When they took a break, I listened intently for Son. There was only a disconcerting silence. I got up and opened the melamine closet. It turned out that the little one had smuggled a heap of little knives into the closet, God only knows how he managed to get hold of them, and while I was watching television, he was cutting his epidermis and his dermis, covering himself with all sorts of sketches.

He sat there and gazed intently at the fine threads of blood oozing out of the cuts. Immediately I dragged him out of the closet, like a midwife delivering a fresh new baby, slapped him hard on both cheeks, and yelled:

"You want me to send you for psychiatric observation? You want to end up crazy so I can have *that* on my wayward conscience too?" The child went berserk, he threw himself on the floor and shrieked like an Arab woman. He knew what was coming. Every time he dared hurt himself, I dumped him directly in a bath of iodine, gave him a tetanus shot, and put him on antibiotics for two months as back-up. When the skinny mite lay in the purple-red bath, up to his neck in the stinging fluid without making a sound, I cupped his tiny head in my hand.

"You can rest assured that your mother takes life seriously," I told him. "That's why you're in there. Is that clear?"

I left him soaking in the iodine for twenty minutes, and by the time I took him out he was swollen with pain. I gave him an analgesic shot and put him to bed in his room, in a sterile plastic tent with filtered air vents.

Although it was eleven o'clock in the morning and other children, maybe not in Dolly City but no doubt in other big cities, were playing on conventional seesaws and swings, I put out the light and shut the door softly behind me, because like it or not—there are some things in life that have to be kept under wraps.

Up to that time my son had never been outside the house in his life, had never seen other children, except on television, which he hated. When I went out for a few hours—very rarely—I put him to sleep. As an educator, I didn't teach him to speak—what for? So he could say "mama?"

When I wasn't rummaging in his insides, I didn't pay attention to him at all. When he sat down opposite me and looked at me sitting, just sitting, facing the window, always facing the window, and him small as a raisin, his hair thin and mangy—I'd tell him to get out of my sight, his watching me got on my nerves. Those eyes—I felt I had to do something about his eyes, maybe sunglasses, maybe tear them out. After all, in Dolly City a sense of hearing is enough to drive you mad, so why burden your mind with visual information too?

Every morning began with a check-up. Every day I concentrated on a different area, in what is called in our jargon "fishing expeditions." My concern for his health knew no bounds. It was voracious, it was grotesque. In the middle of an operation on his leg I would discover problems in the groin. So I would close up the place I'd opened, and open the place that was still closed, and so on and so forth, for hours on end. Until it reached a stage when every inch of his body was open. And then I would pass out.

It was an impossible life, but I lived it nonetheless.

The child was three years old, but he scarcely spoke. His motor development was rudimentary. He was slow, and the only thing he knew how to say was "Don't wanner," instead of "Don't want to."

I stopped going out altogether. Everything over the phone, leave it on the doormat and go, no tip, no nothing. I lived off money I found under the floor tiles, but it too was running out.

Sometimes my mother came to visit. She would look at the child and ask him who his father was. The very posing of this arithmetic problem made my blood boil, and once I took a jar of strawberry jam and smashed it on the floor. Tears flooded my parent's sick eyes, and I asked her to stop it, but she didn't stop it, and then I yelled at her to shut her mouth, and she shut it. I glared at her, and she hugged the child.

The old woman was getting more and more like her mother, the one who'd left me her gold bracelets. Her bones were losing calcium, her eyes were getting smaller, her feet were swelling, her circulation was rotten. Lately she'd been falling down in the street, just collapsing onto all that shit with her bags. She never asked me to have a look at her open wounds, not once. She knew I had troubles of my own, she knew that without my guinea pigs I was lost, that without my diagrams there was nothing for me to do in Dolly City. So she tried to encourage me, to persuade me to get back into the thick of things. Once she brought me a rabbit with leukemia, and once a rheumatic tortoise, together with a few crooked knives she'd picked up in the flea market. Naturally I rejected them out of hand, I had no intention of getting back into all that stuff. I'd seen where it had led me, and decided to leave it alone for the time being. My inactivity upset her. Every day she phoned and asked me:

"What are your plans for today?"

"What are yours?" I asked her. "Have you got any suggestions?"

"I want to buy some soft peaches in the market and bring them for you and the child."

Soft peaches, the old woman was suffering from a soft peaches obsession. She subscribed to all these popular medical journals that I detested. They had charts of vitamins and graphs with longevity on the y-axis. There it said that peaches were good for your blood pressure.

A hard winter came. It rained nonstop, winds blew with a force that swept away thin old men and children suffering from malnutrition. It was freezing cold. The child liked spitting and watching it turn to ice in the air. Apart from which, there was a recession. The trains had almost stopped running. Only the planes were still working, and they were forced to function as land vehicles and transport recruits to their training facilities by coasting along the muddy roads, which soon finished them off.

Due to the situation, my mother sold her house in Hadera and went to live in a trailer car in Rehovot. She told me that I was liable to find myself in the street if I didn't lower my living standard. She advised me to give private lessons in medicine. In these troubled times, she reasoned, no one would bother to check on my papers, and if they did, who'd understand Nepalese anyway?

I took her advice. I opened a course entitled "Introduction to Philanthropic Medicine." I started with three students, and their number grew to fifteen. I was my own boss, nobody asked me what the hell philanthropic medicine was, I could say whatever I liked to my class of ignorant philistines and they swallowed it whole. I exploited the secret desire everyone possesses to be a doctor, to heal, to find a cure for fatal diseases, to lengthen life, to discover the secret of creation.

Sometimes the students would catch a rabbit and bring it upstairs with them, but I would not allow any strange animals on the premises. My guinea pig was therefore the child, who was now already four and a half. I would demonstrate on him, thereby killing two birds with one stone. To attract pupils I started a promotional sale—every third lesson free for anyone who agreed to undergo a simple operation during the course—surgical tooth extraction, liposuction, etc.

I made contact with shady organizations that in exchange for a minimum fee referred manic-depressive personalities to me for surgery. People came. In this manner I performed open-heart surgeries, bypasses, valve replacements, and gave radiation treatments to cancer patients.

Practicing medicine and coming into regular contact with people kept me on an even keel. I no longer occupied myself exclusively with the child. True, I went on opening and closing him like a curtain, but my drive to ascertain that his insides were in order was no longer as strong as it used to be.

In the spring I opened an additional course, in psychiatry.

I accepted only bleeding-heart liberals, or the sort of smug, self-satisfied person who's never even been sodomized. My knowledge of psychiatry is nonexistent, so I really let myself go. I told them all sorts of bullshit, that people can be divided into two classes, those who'd been fucked in the ass and those who hadn't, whether metaphorically or in practice.

The psychiatry course gave me tremendous satisfaction because I really had freedom of action. I did whatever came into my head: I humiliated some people, I exalted others, I poked fun at anyone I felt like poking fun at. I had a ball. I got the biggest kick out of the hypochondriacs. I drove them crazy. I proved to them that they were suffering from several diseases all at once, and that one neutralized the other, with the result that they weren't suffering from anything at all. They didn't know how to take it, so then I said, "Three times a day, before going to bed," and I laughed myself sick.

I discovered a new type of phobia in Dolly City—Arabophobia, fear of Arabs. I had lots of those. The ones with the compulsive fears I harassed the most, because I once read somewhere that you should tackle fear head-on. Fuck Arabs, if you're afraid of them. You fuck them—and you see that the devil's not as black as he's painted, they're just like everybody else.

But one fine day my liberalism was nearly the end of me. I never went into the personal histories of my students, and so, in the middle of performing a gastric bypass on the child, one of my quietest students suddenly stood up, took out a business card, announced that he was a psychiatrist, a graduate of "The Hy and Bye College of Psychiatry, Wimbledon," and demanded that I come with him and be hospitalized, that I undergo in-depth treatment once and for all, and that I place my child in my mother's custody until my soul was healed.

All my life I've run away from psychiatrists as if they were policemen. I threw a couple of chairs and ran down the stairs, and he pursued me with the agility of a grasshopper. Next to the concrete pipes he caught me and gave me an extremely painful shot in the ass. I woke up tied to a bed in a padded room with lichens on the walls, some of them in frames. A very tall orderly came into the room. I showed him my breasts and asked him if he wanted to suck me off. In a second his head was inside me, and I was screaming with pleasure.

My shrieks woke up all the crazy people in the ward, and all of them, men and women, implored the orderly to suck them off too. The orderly really lost it, he didn't know who to suck off first. I took advantage of the uproar to free myself of my bonds, and escaped the insane asylum, because this is the role of loony bins in the world—to provide something to run away from. I didn't return to my apartment, because I knew that was the first place where they would look for me.

I went out to Agrippa Street. The whole street was full of roof-tarrers' signs, and the smell of boiling tar pervaded the air. Busty blondes were stirring the barrels of boiling tar. They all had their hair piled high on their heads, they all had that whole oh-my-lord complex.

And then it hit me: I saw cancerous growths on the blonde women's faces, on the barrels of tar, on the wheels of the buses, on the telephone poles, on the trees, on the wheels of the cars, on the newspapers—wherever I looked, malignant, terminal, spreading tumors danced before my eyes.

I was shaken to the depths of my soul. As a doctor, I knew that it was my duty to treat these tumors, to cut them out, to do something—but I was helpless. Overcome with despair I fell to the ground and closed my eyes, which kept on wanting to open and see the truth—the metastases multiplying in front of them. For half an hour I lay there on the pavement, I could have seen under the horses' tails if only I'd opened my eyes. I could, if I wanted to, have given the horses blowjobs and suckled at the mares' teats.

Eventually I felt better and I sat up. Passersby crossed the long street stretching perpendicular to the sea, where big trees cast their elongated shadows. The cars drove along the wet roads and made a noise like opening a box of wafers. In the sky a flock of seagulls took off, and a blue and white Pan-T plane flying above them entered an air-pocket, but emerged from it heroically.

I raised myself to my feet and dragged myself to the cemetery. I crossed acres in which all the French soldiers who'd died in World War I were buried. Then there were more relevant acres. I reached my father's worn gravestone, and to my amazement I discovered that it too was afflicted by a rare form of cancer. At this point I understood that I'd gotten it bad. I left the graveyard and swooped on everything I came across without exception. I scraped layers of paint off No Parking poles with a Ginsu knife. Everything leapt up and hit me in the eyes, the metastases were taking over the world—it was their finest hour. I stopped passersby and asked them to let me operate on them because they were very, very sick. Only immediate surgical intervention could save them. And I'm a doctor, I told them, and whipped my papers from my pocket. But apart from three nose-less beggars nobody would let me treat them. People were in a terrible hurry. I assaulted a few trees as well, I tore off malignant leaves. The cars had cancer too—skin cancer. I scratched them, collecting samples for biopsies. The whole world was sick, and the entire burden was on my shoulders. I tried everything, God is my witness that I tried to help the cellars and the wine barrels, the drunks and the cripples, the welfare coupons, the purses and the cats. They were all equal in my eyes and they were all very sick.

"You're sick!" I screamed in the streets of Dolly City. "Let me heal you!"

The possibility of saving them all was as remote as five hundred times the distance from Dolly City to the moon. The immensity of the task facing me made me despair.

I hung my head in shame: I was a failure. Everyone was going to die of cancer—and it was all my fault, because I hadn't diagnosed it in time. Afterwards I calmed down a bit. I don't know what calmed me, probably nothing. After the dementia there's always a lull. I bought myself a few chocolate cookies and sat down on a bench to finish them off. I ate with my eyes closed, in order not to see those cancerous worms again.

I tried to accept the situation. I said to myself, okay, Doll, you blew it. Now at least try to alleviate the pain of the world a little, to make it bearable. I patrolled the streets and gave people shots of morphine in the butt. I stood at bus stops and pressed against people like a pickpocket, but I didn't touch their purses. I pressed up against men, they thought I had the hots for them, they started talking dirty, but they had it all wrong. I talked dirty right back, but I stuck my needle into them while I was at it. And I stuck it into tires too. In my heart of hearts I knew that it was complete insanity, that it was a mistake. But I asked myself how

I could be so certain this mistake wasn't really the best solution? My reason countered: How can tires have cancer if they haven't even got leukocytes? I don't know how—but with me it's possible. I told myself that just as human beings can deceive and disguise themselves, so can atoms, molecules, and all the rest. If we can say that the sun is good, that it smiles down on you—how can it also be carcinogenic? But if the sun is carcinogenic, then it's got cancer too.

This was very basic logic, but it was very painful too. I infiltrated the oncology wards of the government hospitals, and stole various analgesics. I made the rounds of the wards, soothing the fatally ill, and went out to the corridor to relieve the suffering of the Arab workers from the Occupied Territories who were cleaning the floor. I didn't discriminate against the mops or the pails either, because nothing human is alien to me.

I knew no rest. My brain worked at the speed of a hurtling train without brakes. My vocation as a doctor destroyed me completely. I took my profession too seriously.

A point of interest: I didn't inject myself. In myself, in my own health, I had complete confidence. Even when I had a fever, I simply jumped into the Thames for a swim or went down to the cellars for a shower. My basic assumption was that I—with my expert understanding of the theory of improbable possibilities—would know if and when cancer caught up with me. And I can say right here and now that even if cancer ever does catch up with me—that's not what this monologue is supposed to be leading up to. No, these are not the confessions of a titless woman.

In November I went to Rehovot to visit my mother. From a distance I could already see that she'd grown even smaller, that yet more calcium had managed to find its way out of her. She was standing in the yard hanging up the laundry, and not far from her, in a big plastic tub, sat the child, surrounded by real, authentic, quacking ducks.

In bygone days this scene would have horrified me, and I could easily have shot my mother for daring to expose my son to the dangers of the world—but now I just grimaced. I waited for my mother to turn her back, whipped out my syringe, and injected the child's bathtub in front of his astonished eyes.

"Stop it, Mom," he said in a tolerant tone.

That was the last straw. I grabbed his head and pushed it into the water so he could see a few fish. I left him with his head underwater for two minutes, he struggled like a chicken in the hands of a butcher. The kid really wanted to live. Suddenly I calmed down. The attack ended as abruptly as it had begun, and I took him out of the water. He was completely blue and his scars were purple.

I left him on the ground, dying, and I knew that I'd just committed the greatest crime a mother, who is also a doctor, can commit. You've been corrupted, Dolly, I said to myself. You made your bed—now lie in it.

The boy lay motionless. I searched for his pulse, but it escaped me like a zebra in the savannah. I didn't have my instruments—I'd left them in a locker at the railway station, but I'd forgotten the number.

I straightened up. I touched his face with the tips of my fingers. It was cold and wet. Underneath my fingers cancer cells were swarming, dividing, and multiplying, multiplying like the abyss that had swallowed me up, and which kept on multiplying itself over and over again as I fell, until I stopped taking any notice of it. Although the child had nearly died of suffocation—I was worried about cancer. My mother emerged from behind a sheet, took in the situation at a glance, and called an ambulance.

"It's insane!" I cried out to her. "To what extremes the female human mind can go, ah, Mother?"

For over an hour the group of doctors tried to resuscitate the child, but it didn't work. I saw that they were on the wrong track. A woman doctor gave him an electric shock. His little body leapt into the air. This was the crucial moment. I couldn't trust anybody.

"Move aside," I cried and pushed my way through, "I'm the mother, and I'm telling you to get out of the way!"

The group of doctors rustled like the wind in a field of thorns, their gowns fluttering on their rigid bodies.

"Get up!" I commanded the child. "Did you hear me? Get up, or I'll take you home!"

"I don't wanner," he said.

"There you are," I said to the startled doctors. "Some children will do anything for attention."

"Strange," said the woman doctor. "There was no pulse. I'm willing to bet a thousand dollars that there was no pulse."

My mother dressed the child, who sat there apathetic and withdrawn. She kissed him. I couldn't stand to see her spoiling him like that—I didn't want him to grow up to be a sissy. But I didn't say anything, because I still doubted he would survive.

I slunk back to Dolly City alone, but when I arrived at my front door, with the intention of jumping straight into bed and for-getting everything—I was astonished to discover that a clan of Kurdish refugees had taken over my apartment. Everybody in Dolly City knows that you can't argue with the Gypsy or the Kurdish refugees or with Asians either. They're terribly sensitive, they can't tolerate any kind of remark or criticism, and you just have to leave them alone.

"Excuse me," I said, "many years ago I used to live here. Can I just come in for a minute and look around? Thank you so much."

The Kurds were sitting in the Jacuzzi and using my shampoo. In the bedroom I saw the maniac psychiatrist who hospitalized me fucking one of the refugees. I came closer, they were in the throes of passion, the psychiatrist was busy cursing all the women in the world, calling them whores and saying that they should all have their clitorises and breasts cut off to teach them a lesson and put them in their place. He noticed me and wasn't in the least sur-prised to see me there.

"Dolly," he said, "did they give you a vacation? How are you? What was your week like? How is the treatment progressing?"

"As planned," I replied, whipped one of my knives out from my belt, and castrated him. What I'd done to my animals dozens of times—I now did for the first time to a living man, and I have to say that it was worth every minute.

"Now, you son of a bitch, go and get hormone treatments in Bangladesh, and next time call your mother a whore."

I smiled at the woman, but she wasn't interested. She pounced on the amputated member and went on pursuing her romance with it as if nothing had happened, and I thought to myself that the real problem with most people, including me, was that they were so sickeningly thorough. It was this damn sense of responsibility that drove them insane.

The eunuch's eyes rolled around in his head, he screamed, and jumped out of the window.

It was night, the last night of October. The moon and the stars were sprinkled over the sky like salt on wounds. Desperate men fucked tree trunks.

I arrived at a big toy shop. It was full of mothers buying their children Circassian dolls that could easily be taken apart and put together again. Six months had passed since I tried to drown my son, but also six months since I'd brought him back to life, depending on exactly when you start counting. That, by the way, was the last time I'd seen him.

A saleslady in a brown dress came up to me. I averted my eyes and pretended to be looking at something else. I didn't have the money for a Circassian doll, so I attached myself to a tall woman holding one.

"Quick!" I cried when I caught up with her, "Over there!" and I pointed to one of the skyscrapers, "A child! He's about to fall!"

She screamed and dropped the Circassian doll. I picked up my loot and ran to catch the fast train to Rehovot. It rained all the way. The train traveled so fast I could hardly breathe, but everybody behaved completely normal.

My mother opened the door almost immediately, her hair as pale as her lips, and her face wrinkled and tired. Behind her, on a little rug, the child was playing with wooden blocks. It was dark, I didn't know what to say. I said:

"Hi, Mother. You've aged. Your hair's gone all white. Your face is wrinkled. You look awful. Would you like me to give you a face-lift?"

She stretched her lips in a kind of smile and opened the door wide. Son looked at me. His eyes went blank, and he returned to his blocks.

"Say hello to mommy," said my mother.

"I don't wanner," said the boy.

"You don't wanner?" I said. "Can't you say I don't want to? Want to? Want to?" I yelled. "I'll show you!" The blood almost burst out of my skull from rage.

I grabbed hold of a bamboo carpet-beater, brandished it in the air, and brought it down with all my strength on the child, but he managed to escape in the nick of time. My mother jumped on me and tried to wrest the carpet-beater from my hands.

"Don't interfere between a mother and her son," I snapped. "Ever!"

"But you're my daughter!" she cried.

"Can't you understand anything?" I said. As I was struggling with her, with Son sniggering in the distance, she suddenly froze in her spot and fell to the floor of the RV. I dropped the carpet-beater and bent over her.

"Call the doctor," she murmured. "I'm not feeling so well."

"What's the matter with you? Have you forgotten that I'm a doctor? Tell me, where does it hurt?"

"Even Napoleon thought he was Napoleon," she said, and the kid sprinkled cold water onto her pale face from the palm of his hand. She recovered and sat up, and he returned to his blocks.

"Why does everyone always pick on Napoleon?" I said, overcome by weakness, and fell into a chair. "Why?"

"What's that?" she pointed to the parcel containing the doll.

"It's for him," I confessed. The kid stood up and approached me cautiously. I saw that he was afraid of me, so I rolled the doll towards him.

"Open it, open the present, kid," I told him.

He pulled the colored ribbons and looked at the doll with interest.

"What is it?" he asked.

"A Circassian doll," I said.

"Chocolate?" he asked.

"A Circassian doll, you pest."

"Candy?" he asked.

"A Circassian doll—"

"French fries?"

"What's the matter with you? Are you deaf? Dyslexic? Couldn't you teach him to talk like a human being?" I reproached my mother, who was ironing a shirt in a corner of the RV.

"Are you still seeing tumors everywhere?" she asked me.

"Believe me when I say that I don't know exactly what I'm seeing anymore," I said, and she nodded. "Not always," I began trying to answer her question again, "sometimes all I see is swelling. Things swell up out of all proportion. I have a problem with the process of growth. I suppose I have a problem with the process of life. I don't know. Either I see red," I narrowed my eyes, "or I see black. Lately I've been seeing flies in the pupils of people's eyes, the pupils of butterflies' eyes, in the pupils, pupils—believe me, I don't know why I should be so stuck on pupils." I fell silent and rubbed my treacherous eyes.

"Tell me, dear, maybe you just need eyeglasses? Maybe after all these years your vision has simply weakened?"

"Bullshit," I snapped. "Can't you see that glasses aren't my problem?"

She went back to her ironing in silence, and I watched a talk show on TV.

"Pardon me, Doll," the old woman said warily, "what do you mean, you see red, you see black?"

"It's more like a red spot, the memory of a spot, as if the color didn't have enough exposure to the eyes, and only the brain managed to perceive it somehow."

"Look at me, my daughter," she said, straightening up and setting the iron on its aluminum base, "do you see red and black spots on my face?"

"Yes," I replied. "And on him too. He's got a rash. Maybe it's a childhood disease, maybe it's the beginning of leukemia. Come here, come here." The old woman tensed and leapt to the defense of the child.

"Leave him alone, he hasn't got a rash."

"Don't you understand, stupid? Can't you see? The child's got a rash, he's going to die, get out of my way," I gave her a shove. "Show me your vein," I said to the kid, "show me your stomach, pull your shirt up. I don't know, has he got a rash, Mother? Come and look, I don't know what I'm seeing any more."

The woman shot me a hostile look.

"Do me a favor, look at him, do me a favor."

"He hasn't got a rash, his skin is completely white."

"In my opinion he's got smallpox. Didn't I inoculate him against smallpox?" I asked myself aloud.

"There's no smallpox in Rehovot," said the old woman in a stern voice, picked the child up in her arms, and carried him to the far end of the trailer. I followed her. I was having a severe fit.

"Give me the child," I said. "I have to take blood."

"You're not touching the child."

"I have to count his leukocytes, to see if he needs antibiotics."

"To count his what?"

"The child has to get a few days' sick leave, he's got to be in an isolation room."

"What sick leave are you talking about? What isolation room? The child's five years old!"

"In Staff HQ," I said coldly.

"But the child," cried my mother, "is only a child! What are you talking about, Staff HQ?"

"Yes, I suppose you have a point," I said.

"You don't say!" cried my mother, but I took no notice of her.

"I have to make sure he won't be fit for combat . . ."

"Get out of here!" shrieked my mother. "I never want to see you again. You're no daughter of mine. *Inti majnuna*, you're out of your mind!"

"Give me the child," I said, and she shook her head hysterically.

"Over my dead body, over my dead . . ."

Don't worry—I didn't kill her, I just put her to sleep. I grabbed hold of the kid's arm, I was about to cut it with a kitchen knife, but suddenly I asked myself a simple question: how was I planning to count the leukocytes, without any measuring instruments? A cool breeze of sanity blew through me and told me that if the child had leukemia, he would certainly have other symptoms, and if he had smallpox, then sooner or later he would die or recover, at which point these two possibilities, that he would either die or recover, somehow seemed less overwhelming, and I decided that maybe I was cuckoo, maybe my mind was as shaky as a rotten wooden bridge over the source of the Thames—but he was my son, for better or worse, in sanity or insanity, and I was taking him home to Dolly City.

All the way back to town the child lay with his head on my lap, and I picked out his lice and squished them with my fingers. Even inside the train people kept on moving, the movement of the train wasn't enough for them, the rattle of the rails, the revolutions of the earth weren't enough for them, they had to keep passing from one coach to another, and to get up all the time to go to the lavatory, open and close the windows, change seats, anything to keep moving.

No one in Dolly City rolled out a red carpet for us, no one welcomed us home. People were in a hurry to arrive, to catch the last train, because all the trains in Dolly City were the last ones, all of them thought they were more last than the others.

I saw malignant tumors on the Saint Bernard dogs, on the barbed wire, on my child's head. He had brown spots on his hands, moles sprouted all over him, he was covered with a horrifying neon rash, and he limped too, he had rheumatic fever. I had already made up my mind to resign myself to the cancer of the environment and concentrate on the cancer of my son, to take care of him and only him—and the rest of the world could die and burn in hell.

I bought a pair of binoculars and went into an old laundry. I planned to look at my child through them, maybe I'd see something I hadn't seen before. A teacher of medicine in Katmandu had once told us, his students, that sometimes, in making a diagnosis, you should step back and look at things from a distance through binoculars. I sat the kid with the Circassian doll on a dryer (closed, the door of the dryer was closed), took several steps backwards, aimed, and locked in on the target.

I couldn't tell my ass from my elbow, and I realized that it must be set for greater distances, or else my binoculars were fucked.

"Sit there, and don't touch anything," I warned the kid and went outside. It was peak hour, and a million people were going in and out of the subway stations, walking past the obscene graffiti on the walls like on any other day without blinking an eye. They were in such a hurry that they even continued walking on the escalators, onwards and upwards. I found an optician's shop. I went in and persuaded the optician to come with me and enlighten me on the mysteries of the binoculars I'd bought. I led her to the laundry, and while I was busy explaining the problem in all its details, I located a malignant growth on her neck, and cut short my explanation in order to inform her that it was the end of her, but she didn't care. She declared that life had to go on whatever happened, took my binoculars apart, and told me that it was trash.

"What do you mean?" I asked, but she didn't reply.

"Who's that?" she inquired, looking at the boy.

"My son."

"What does he want?"

"Just to live, I suppose."

"Did you ask him?"

"He hardly talks, he's very problematic."

"What do you mean, he doesn't talk, is he dumb?"

"He can't get the words out. Do I have to come up with an explanation for everything?"

"What a strange woman you are," she said.

"If one of us is strange, it's probably you," I said.

"Me? What's your name?" she asked with a pretence of friendliness.

"Dolly."

"Dolly. Is that short for Dikla?"

"It's an acronym. And what's your name?"

"Ninette Oberzon. An acronym of what?"

"Aren't you tired?" I asked her, hoping she'd get the hint. She yawned and said: "No. Actually," she said as she yawned again, "I can't keep my eyes open," and her eyes closed, she lay down on the floor, put her head on a pile of dirty underwear, and fell asleep. The child's face was swept with terror, he feared what was to happen next, and with good reason.

I picked up Ninette Oberzon, put her into the washing machine, and pressed the "Start" button.

Dolly City, a city without a base, without a past, without an infrastructure. The most demented city in the world. All the people in Dolly City are usually on the run. Since they're always running, there's always someone chasing them, and since there's someone chasing them, they catch them and execute them and throw them into the river. The trains in Dolly City run like runs in panty-hose—if you don't stop them, they'll reach your crotch. Dolly City, a city of intensive traffic—in everything, babies included. All the babies in Dolly City are adopted, the little bastards. All the mothers in Dolly City are fucked up, screwed up. All the trains in Dolly City rattle nonstop. The regime in Dolly City is democratic, however ridiculous it may sound, Dolly City is a democracy. There are two big parties: Bureaucracy and Procedure. The parties each have gangs of street kids who take the law into their own hands. The soldiers of the Bureaucracy party are the Trashers. Revolting, dirty, unhygienic types, who spend all their time pickpocketing, coughing, wiping their noses on their sleeves, and relieving themselves in their pants. A Trasher never says hello, he only acts—they especially like to spray graffiti on walls where there's a strong smell of male urine.

The Trashers mainly eat easily digested fish, or tuna mousse. On the other hand, the Alrighters of the Procedure party are an entirely different kettle of fish. They're all right—absolutely, gorgeously all right. Every one of the Alrighters has swum across the Kinnereth dozens of times. They all adore hiking in Jerusalem, most of them go jogging round the Old City walls every evening. Most of the Alrighters polish diamonds and sing wonderful songs in the shower. They know all the great, old Hebrew songs, including, "Oh, the garden of sycamore trees, oh-ho."

There are gangs in Dolly City too, like the Apostrophes, whose slogan is as dumb as their faces. They sing to a Reggae beat: "The state is me / Please decapitate me." And then there are the Cowards, the Archetypes, and the Bonbons, but most of the inhabitants of Dolly City belong to the category of "like-thats," because of the line, "There were people like that, too, a long time ago," from the song, "Oh, the garden of sycamore trees, oh-ho . . ." The "like-thats" are the descendants of ancient and enthusiastic woodcutters who suffered from hyperactivity, and cut down all the trees around their houses simply for the sake of having something to take their aggression out on.

Luckily for me, I managed to avoid falling into any of these groups—I learned to keep a low profile. I learned that the trick is simply to pretend to be asleep, and so clandestinely undermine.

So—we found ourselves in the streets, me and the child. We slept, like most of the homeless, in filthy niches, in buses, in abandoned train coaches. The usual bullshit of life went on. That whole shtick of day following night, with the seasons also doing their best to take over one from another, if not always with notable success.

I forbade the child to touch me, or enter my field of vision, because I would immediately have discovered a tumor and been obliged to operate, and I no longer had the instruments or the right conditions, and to be honest I'd begun to detest these Sisyphean operations, I was just plain sick and tired of them.

I went to an old carpenter and asked him to glue the child to my back. First of all, I wouldn't see him, and because of the layer of glue I wouldn't actually touch him either. Secondly, he would grow on my back, and gradually he would become part of me, and I would become part of him, and then, when the barriers between us broke down completely, I would be able to incorporate him inside myself and forget all about him, and I wouldn't have to worry so much anymore. As for the not particularly aesthetic hump, I didn't give a damn, I knew that anyone who wanted me would take me as I was, and if my hump bothered him—let him go fuck somebody else.

As soon as I emerged from the carpenter's moldy den, another ghastly accident took place. A train was derailed, the coaches turned over, two hundred people were crushed to death, and the wounded screamed under the wreckage.

I looked at this familiar scene, and wondered how many times in human history people had been buried under the ruins of something which they themselves had built. I addressed myself to the task of tending the wounded. My son—as if the carpenter's glue wasn't enough for him—hugged me tightly, and this made me panic, I was afraid that before I knew what hit me he would plant a kiss on me—and a kiss meant cancer of the teeth, the mouth, and the gums. Apart from which, my back was itching like hell.

I leaned over a severely wounded man. He implored me to amputate his foot, and I asked him to scratch my back in return. We made a deal, I lay down on my stomach in the middle of a sewage canal, my chin right in the shit and my nose getting a hell of a whiff, and the bearded, wounded man pushed a twig into the narrow space that the carpenter had omitted to smear with his carpenter's glue, and scratched and rubbed, and asked: "Is that better? Is that better?"

"Yes, that's better," I said.

We went—or so I thought—our separate ways, but half an hour later, when I stopped to take a leak, I saw the man with the amputated foot walking behind me, if you could call those crooked hops walking. I stamped my foot to chase him away. You take a person's foot, and they want to give you their whole leg. I threw stones at him, let him go somewhere else, let him pose as a wounded war veteran, let him collect Social Security—what did he want from me?

"What do you want?" I asked him eventually.

But the leech didn't reply. I crossed roads, walked across bridges, went up and down on escalators—and he kept on following me.

"What do you want?" I asked him again.

"I want to show you something."

"I'll see everything in hell when I get there."

"No, no, please, you must. I want to show you something."

I gave in and followed him. For half an hour we proceeded in silence, and then the man entered the courtyard of an abandoned building, made his way to the far end, opened a creaking wooden door, and pointed to a few plants growing on the ground.

"What's that?"

"My garden."

"Is that what you brought me here for?"

"Yes."

"Do I look like a psychiatrist? You think I've got time for your nonsense? Go to hell."

"Go to hell and get fucked yourself."

"Fuck you, and your father too."

The man smiled, held out his calloused brown hand and said: "My name's Gordon. I'm the first Jew to work the land since the destruction of the Second Temple."

"Scratch Gordon." It slipped out.

"I grow organic vegetables. I thought, for the child perhaps, that you might want organic vegetables."

The man stuck to me like a leech. Wherever I went he followed me with his organic vegetables. Apparently he'd succeeded in planting vegetables in various places in Dolly City and growing them without any chemical agents. Looking back, he was a pest, but at the time—not that I'd actually converted to his ideas—I let him talk. The only thing I censored was his tendency to sing in the evenings: "How lovely are the nights in Canaan."

He took an interest in me and the child. He asked questions about his educational upbringing. He inquired as to what school of thought I belonged. "No school," I said.

"Only the earth," he said after hearing a bit of the child's history. "Only Mother Earth. You're a bundle of nerves. You belong in the earth. You have to find the roots of your soul, you have to dig for them. Who knows," he said in a different, reflective tone, "maybe you'll discover that you're the child's real mother . . ."

"That I'm this child's real mother?"

"Perhaps."

"Then who's the father?"

"The father's less important. A child needn't know who his father is, but a child who doesn't know who his mother is—that's serious."

"And what about the video of the bris? What about the hidden connection between him and the Pan-T pilots, especially one specific pilot and his daughter?"

"You know what," he frowned, "you pay too much attention to details. You should take a more global view of things. You think I haven't got cracks in my memory? You have to resign yourself to the existence of illogical, uncertain elements. Look at me, I'm sixty-seven years old, and I'm not afraid to die because I'm not afraid of Mother Earth. I've cultivated her all my life, and in the end she'll reward me when she becomes my eternal resting place. Like the fruits of the earth, Dolly, when I ripen—I'll drop from the tree like a guava on the eve of Sukkot."

Gordon and I learned firsthand that wandering through Dolly City was far more horrible than wandering through anywhere else. Better do it in cities like Rome, Paris, or Katmandu, if you must. All we did in life was try to stay alive. We just soldiered on.

And winter came again. The child was cold as iron. Snowflakes caught on Gordon's gray beard, snow whitened his gardens, and he, with his inner serenity, cleared the snow from his strawberry beds and shook the flakes off the frozen child.

Gordon felt connected to the history of the world, especially the history of the Jews. He drew me out a little, and I told him about all kinds of things that I'd done. I toned down the tales of my cruelty, but I think he understood. He even suggested that I write down the names of all the people I'd killed in my life in a notebook, dividing the page into columns: one for those I'd killed out of negligence, one for those I'd killed by mistake, and one for those I'd harpooned with everything I had. One day he even bought me a notebook, but I left it lying on the bench.

In the course of one of our heart-to-hearts, on the banks of the frozen river, warming ourselves at the flames of a campfire he'd lit, he asked me: "Tell me, Doctor Dolly, why didn't you study medicine at the University of Tel Aviv? Why did you go all the way to Nepal?"

"Why did I go all the way to Nepal?"

"Why did you go all the way to Nepal."

"I'll tell you why, I had a free ticket, the last free ticket my father, who was a Pan-T employee, managed to get for me before he died. On his last night in the Ichilov Hospital, in the oncology ward, he murmured to me with the voice of a dying man, 'Oh, Dolly, you have no *objectif* in life. You're just drifting, it's insufferable. Study something, study medicine, study medicine in Katmandu for all I care, as long as you study.' "

"Aha," said Gordon, "so he was the one who put that ridiculous idea in your head."

"You could say that."

"But you know, Dolly," he said, and threw another twig onto the fire, where it was immediately welcomed with jolly crackles by its burning friends, "can't you tell the difference between something said seriously and something said metaphorically? Your father may he rest in peace didn't actually mean that you should go and study in Katmandu. He meant . . ."

"How do you know what he meant?" I interrupted him. "How the hell does anybody know what he meant?" I was terribly offended. The thought that my father hadn't actually intended me to go and study medicine in Katmandu was devastating, since this was the first and last thing he'd told me to do that I actually did. Gordon noticed my agitation and stopped talking. After all, he too hadn't gotten off lightly in life. His worship of the earth and its fruits had made him lose his sense of proportion. Instead of shooting up heroine, he injected himself with chlorophyll, but it didn't have any effect because it was just chlorophyll, there was nothing narcotic about it. He was convinced that it did something for him, and I didn't want to spoil his high.

He decided that I didn't have a clear enough idea of my identity, and he drilled me by asking me questions:

"Name please."

"Dolly."

"Occupation?"

"Doctor."

"Family situation?"

"X plus child."

"What's X plus child?"

"I don't know, it just came out."

"Profession?"

"Doctor."

"Hobbies?"

"Medicine, biology, zoology, pathology."

"Parents?"

"Two."

"What do you mean two?"

"Father, mother. Two."

"Origins of parents?"

"Nile River, next to the delta," I said carefully. He smiled.

"Education?"

"Whose? My parents'?"

"Yours."

"Medicine. I'm a doctor. I studied medicine in Katmandu, Nepal."

"Place of residence?"

"Dolly City. That's enough. I've had enough of this nonsense. Stop it."

For six months we dragged our asses from place to place. Our walks got more and more depressing and made us both wish we were dead. Once I nearly jumped into the Thames with my child, who kept on growing on my back. If it weren't for Gordon, I would have put an end to it long ago. With the child. Without the child. Without the child, because he might have kept me afloat like swimmies and saved my life.

Toward the end, things didn't go too smoothly. The atmosphere between us became heavy. But we still managed to get through to each other.

Once Gordon succeeded in persuading me to shoot up with chlorophyll. He told me it was a thousand times more natural than those yellow antidepressants I'd been swallowing for fifteen years.

"It's organic," he said. "It can only do you good." And it was really something—if it was anything at all.

He succeeded in persuading me to shoot chlorophyll, and I succeeded in persuading him that it was possible that telephone poles had cancer.

Maybe five times I found myself tripping on chlorophyll. Once, Gordon, who was also high on the stuff, said let's go to a strip show. It really freaked me out, that the old man wanted to see strippers. When we went into the show in the November Club, he didn't take his eyes off the fig leaf covering the girl's crotch. Afterwards it turned out that it was the fig leaf that turned him on, not what was underneath it, because when she removed the leaf, and all the men filled their undies with their mango juice, Gordon went for the green leaf, which he put into his mouth and chewed.

One day he said:

"Doctor, I think I've put my finger on your problem. You think your child's made of sponge, and that eighty percent of him is water. You think your child's a sliced-up watermelon. The child is not a watermelon. Get that into your head."

"Gordon, my head's already full to bursting."

"Full of shit, that's what it's full of—shit!"

"So?"

"You're a blasphemer. That's what you are. If you weren't a blasphemer, you would never have come to the conclusion that your son is a watermelon and that eighty percent of him is water in the first place."

"I'm a blasphemer? You know, you're not the first person who's ever called me a blasphemer."

"You doubt creation. That's the heart of the matter. Let God do his job. Why are you interfering? You don't trust God. Just look at the world, it's all handmade. Just look. Black and white, yellow and orange—it's all the work of one God."

"I don't trust God?" I was offended.

"No."

"It's God who doesn't trust me," I said.

"You're a fool," said Gordon. "You're driving up a one-way street in the wrong direction."

"I don't get it."

"So you don't get it, so what? So you don't get it. So you're dumb. And that's that."

"I don't understand you, Gordon. All the streets in Dolly City are one-way streets, but everybody drives in all directions anyway—that's the main reason for the chaos!"

"You're a fool."

"I'm not a fool."

"You're a fool."

"You're a fool!"

"Me?"

"Yes, you. Why don't you build yourself a ghost town of your own?"

"Why don't I build myself a ghost town of my own. An excellent question."

He sank into thought, while I passed the child a few tablets of pressed wheat.

"Why don't I build myself a ghost town of my own . . ." repeated Gordon after half an hour.

I sighed.

"Maybe you don't want to build yourself a ghost town, but a ghost village. Are you with me?"

"Yes, I'm with you," he said, but it wasn't true. For a few weeks already I'd noticed he was changing. He hardly slept and spent whole nights sitting motionless at the edge of the canal.

"When I die—" he suddenly said one evening, "will they really bury me in the Rishon LeZion wine cellars, like it says in the song?"

"What?" I was startled.

"I don't want to be buried in the Rishon LeZion wine cellars. Can they force me?"

I didn't say anything. History and folklore had taken him over completely. All his theories about Mother Earth and working the land were bullshit. He was just an intellectual the entire time.

We parted after about nine months on the roads together. He said that he was sick of Dolly City, he wanted to try his luck in Mexico City.

"You're unhappy in Dolly City . . ." I said, overcome by melancholy. Dolly City was indeed one big grave.

"Dolly City," he said, "is not a place to put down roots or start a farm. It's not a place. It's an ugly, disgusting, stinking, filthy, boring, depressing town—what else is there to say?"

"So," I said, deeply offended, "you're getting out?"

"Aha."

And he left. He stopped a truck, got on, and it drove off. And I went back to town.

PART THREE

A few months before my father kicked the bucket, a few months before the doctors came to the conclusion that he was on his way out, one of the medical giants who was treating him, a long-faced specialist from the outpatient lung clinic at Ichilov, had a sudden revelation and sent him to the pain clinic on Henrietta Szold, the parallel street.

"There's nothing the matter with you. Apart from a terrible pain in the left side of the lung. It's nothing, it's nerves, pure nerves."

For three months, every Tuesday or Wednesday, my father showed up at the pain clinic, and week after week one of the not-quite-doctors there took a huge needle and stuck it in his back, brutalizing one of the nerves. The not-quite's hobby was killing nerves in cancerous bodies. The hobby of his colleague, that first not-quite, was convincing the patients to kill off the nerve.

Up until then I'd never heard of this genre of physicians—the not-quite-doctors, who aren't exactly doctors and aren't exactly quacks, but something in between. From what I gathered, these characters smile easily, their touch is warm and pleasant, the color of their skin is grayish-brown, and they speak good Hebrew and passable English.

These two not-quites led my dying father up the garden path. Three days after this nerve-killing ritual, during the course of which my father convinced himself that the pain had gone—it came back, bigger than ever. The not-quite-doctors attacked the nerve with their injections about twenty-five times. They had a full-scale strategy, they marked black dots on my father's back with all kinds of special pencils, they stuck compasses into his back and drew circles on it, God knows why. And my father, that poor sucker, would sit there without saying a word and submit to their treatment, which had no affect at all on his agonizing pains, against which I myself waged a failing campaign by telling him he was only imagining them.

Only after three months of barren treatment—I remember, it was the middle of summer, the three acacia trees in the empty lot across the street were green, the bus was carting away the excrement of the North Tel Aviv suburb—my father sat in a rocking chair, and told me that he knew he had cancer, that he only went to the pain clinic for the fun of it, and that when a doctor told you there was nothing wrong with you, it was a sure sign you were going to die.

I sat on the bench with my fat ass spilling in all directions, with the kid stuck on my back preventing me from leaning properly against it, and asked myself if I shouldn't open a pain clinic like the one in Henrietta Szold, in other words, with the main idea behind the treatment being to concentrate exclusively on the pain, and not on its causes. About three years earlier, when I lost my marbles and saw malignant tumors everywhere, back then I'd also concentrated on the pain, but that was out of distress, out of compulsion, whereas now we were talking about an entirely new conception I've embraced.

As a beginning, to get some ideas, I went to Henrietta Szold Street in Dolly City. I assumed that if there was a Henrietta Szold Street in Tel Aviv, there would be one in Dolly City too, between Ichilov and the Haifa expressway. I did find the street, but I didn't find a pain clinic. In the place where the clinic should have been, there was a brothel run by a few Kurdish refugees who'd moved in and taken over.

I went to Gare Saint-Lazare. I assumed that if there was a Gare Saint-Lazare in Paris, then there would be one in Dolly City too, but there wasn't anything that came anywhere near it. Instead I found another brothel run by Kurdish refugees.

I returned to the main street, deep in thought, wondering how I was going to adapt my program to the existing circumstances. I went into a brothel and asked the madam, who was actually a man, to give me a shot so that I could use the money to establish a pain-relief stall. I asked for something clean and easy. She understood right away and fixed me up with someone who only wanted to rub against me. I didn't understand exactly what he had in mind, and it took me a while to realize that that was all there was to it. He just walked past me and rubbed against me slightly with his leg, continued to the end of the room, took out a few bills, and left.

I waited for a day and a half at the Dolly City city hall for a license to open a stall, until in the end they informed me that it was out of the question and impossible. I found a piece of cardboard and wrote on it: "Soother: Instant Relief from Your Pain." I said to myself, you see, Dolly, all you have to do with your ideas is institutionalize them. A few years ago you ran around Dolly City with a syringe, injecting everyone you came across with painkillers, and now you're doing the same thing—but you're earning a living at it.

I drugged people. When I couldn't get hold of sedatives or analgesics I injected them with Pepsi-Cola, and I have no idea what it did to them. A lot of Pan-T flight attendants and air-crew personnel came to me directly from their flights so I'd stick it in their backsides. They suffered from migraines due to stress. Quite a few pilots suffering from lower-back pains came too. They came dressed in their pilots' uniforms and behaved as if the whole world was supposed to lick their boots. I got rid of them real quick, I couldn't stand the smell of their aftershave.

I had another reason for keeping them at arm's length: I was afraid one of them might recognize his grandson on my back. But my fears were superfluous. After everything he'd been through, the child looked like nobody but himself. To be exact, he looked like a ghost, and passersby would stop in the street to stare at him as if he were a freak of nature. Some of them made fun of him too, and I let them, so he wouldn't get too spoiled, so he'd know that this world was a hospital for the mentally ill.

My son would see the hostile looks and roar like a tiger with an arrow stuck in its chest, hours would pass before he'd begin to cry, and then another few hours until he'd calm down.

I accumulated hundreds of hours of injections, but gradually people either died or got used to living with the pain, and my business started rapidly deteriorating. The state of my finances was in deep shit. In order to go on breathing the salty air of Dolly City, I was obliged to take up euthanasia—the branch of medicine I hate the most, because it's neither one thing nor the other. It's not murder, and it's not saving lives—so what is it? It's the moment when medicine admits failure. I hated killing off terminal geriatric cases—even more than a dentist hates pulling a tooth that he could have saved if he'd seen it a few years earlier.

I got fed up with euthanasia. I went into sexual diseases. I kept it up for two months. For a while I walked around with a sign saying that I was a gynecologist, and when I was sick of that, I became an ear-nose-and-throat specialist. For months I kept at it like a yo-yo. I wandered from field to field, from specialization to specialization, like the Israelites wandering from place to place throughout the long years of their exile.

After that I took a rest from medicine for a while. I couldn't take it anymore, my doubtful diagnoses were coming out of my ears. Maybe if I'd been a doctor with a clinic and business cards and white coats, maybe then I could have carried on, but this hand-to-mouth medicine was killing me as well as my patients. I found a job in the cemetery as an usher, taking the mourners to the grave and showing them the quickest way out. But it bored me stiff, and I gave it up after a week.

I might as well take the opportunity to say a couple of things about madness here. Beyond any doubt—madness is a predator. Its food is the soul. It takes over the soul as rapidly as our forces occupied Judea, Samaria, and the Gaza Strip in 1967. After madness takes over and settles in the territory of the human mind, the mad cows come into the picture. All they know to do is eat, so they stuff themselves sick and lay the fields waste. And if a state like the State of Israel can't control the Arabs in the territories, how can anybody expect me, a private individual, to control the occupied territories inside myself?

And once I'm on the subject of politics, I'd like to ask, why don't the Americans bomb Dolly City? They've got atomic weapons! Why don't a few enlightened nations get together and blast this wretched city right off the map?

After humanity succeeds in finding a cure for cancer, it will have to devote itself to finding a way to kill madness without killing the madman with it.

I went into a pub. A blonde singer was singing, "Electricity flows through your fingertips." I wanted to lie down on the table and say: Okay, okay, let's have the shock treatment, even though it doesn't help, it doesn't help. The kid was turned on by the music, he began jumping up and down and going berserk on my back, I wanted to turn around and whop him one.

In the middle of the night they closed the pub, and I went outside with a piece of cheesecake in my hand. I ate the cheesecake. It was my eighth or ninth slice, I was so fat I could hardly walk. The pregnancy on my back didn't make life any easier either, to put it mildly. I lay down on a stone bench on my stomach, above a column of black ants, and tried to remember the last time I had lain on my back. I thought to myself that I must be about thirty-six, if not more, and I calculated that the kid must be six years old by now, and maybe the time had come to detach him from my back and send him on his way. Let him get on with his life. As far as I was concerned, let him hang some ugly sign on his transparent chest and beg for money in the street, and I'd be able to lie on my back in peace.

I found a store that sold everything. I went inside, and asked if they would get the child off my back. They looked at me suspiciously, and asked me why, since the child was young and weak. I said that I only wanted a few days without a sack of flour on my back. Just a few days, and after that I'd stick him back on again. They agreed. I lay on my stomach for half a day until they managed to get him off my back without tearing any skin off him or me. They proceeded millimeter by millimeter, and all the time they kept saying that they didn't understand why I was putting in all this effort if I intended to stick him back on in a week's time.

They finished the job. I threw a few coins on the wooden table and went outside. I planned to give him the slip. Let him go, let him get on with it, leave me alone. We reached the anti-anti-Semite quarter of town, where the holocaust survivors crucify a different goy every day. They were just crucifying a Finnish carpenter. He begged them to spare him, but after all, their parents didn't want to die either.

The kid was fascinated, and I disappeared on him. I hid behind a pillar to see how he was getting on. One part of me said: Run away, Dolly, disappear, but another part told me not to move. For an hour and a half my son bawled, until I stepped out. As soon as he saw me, he ran towards me, but I averted my eyes. The kid looked bad. He was the reflection of the madness of years. I told him to walk a meter or two behind me and to do his best to avoid his reflection in mirrors or shop windows.

We reached Milano Square. I lay down on the green grass opposite the Milano Café and looked up at the blue sky. The kid popped up in my field of vision, luckily for him the sun was in my eyes.

"What do you want?" I asked him.

"I feel sick."

He was weak, he couldn't walk. He lay down next to me, and I opened my bag and told him to turn over and lie on his stomach. I wanted to bring the map I had drawn on his back all those years ago up to date, to enlarge it in accordance with the child's growth, and to color the green line an olive-green.

He lay on his stomach until I was finished. In the end I contemplated the map, with all that Lebanon, those cedars of Lebanon, and all those Jordan Valley rifts, all those lofty peaks, and swamps drained by pioneers, and Kiryat Shmoneh, where I had an albino cousin who once spat at me, and Arad, where I had another cousin, and suddenly an idea came into my head, I looked at the razzle-dazzle all around me, and I said to myself: Dolly, an exhibition! With this map as one of the exhibits.

I was filled with joy and a certain feeling of anticipation. I opened my portfolio and took out all kinds of things I'd done over the years. There were sketches from Katmandu and all kinds of instruments, and I arranged everything in a row, more or less. I called my exhibition "Forte Depressione."

I surveyed my exhibits and smiled. Men and gentlemen rushed past me frantically to catch the last train, casting a glance at this display of mine as they ran, but some of them stopped and looked at my exhibition with disgust.

"You want to buy?" I asked, and pointed to one of the more interesting heads in my collection, but the repressed inhabitants of Dolly City looked at my treasures with a vacant stare.

Only one of them, dressed in a toady-green leather jacket, examined my exhibition with interest, and in the end he said:

"One thing I can say for you, ma'am, you're not trying to bribe God . . ."

"You're right," I replied. "I'm not trying to bribe God. I'm only trying to keep the devil at bay."

"What's that?" he inquired, pointing to a limp arm tattooed with a concentration camp number.

"That's part of life," I replied.

"Don't get smart with me," he said. "Just tell me—"

"Only if you buy it."

"I'll buy it."

I dropped my eyes.

"That's the arm of my elementary school teacher. I met her recently in the streets of Dolly City. She didn't recognize me, but I recognized her all right. I offered to give her an enema. She looked at me with revulsion." I was silent for a moment. "I hated her. She made me ashamed of not being the daughter of holocaust survivors. Because of her I was ashamed that my uncles weren't murdered by the Nazis, but are all alive and kicking in Kiryat Ata."

"And that?" he pointed to another exhibit.

"That's my brother who never existed. He died in the Yom Kippur War. On the first day of the war."

"I don't understand. If he never existed in the first place, how did he die?"

"It's a little difficult to explain," I said uneasily. "And those," I pointed to a bit of hair, "are the remains of my father's moustache. He had a moustache. I tried to get hold of his mother's bones too, they say she's buried in Gaza. He had four sisters, all four of them died of different diseases before they were twenty-five. My father never said a word about them. His mother died of a broken heart. She gave birth to my father and put an end to it. They say that her husband was the death of her. He's buried in Haifa. I've never seen his grave . . ."

I went into a little café. It was one o'clock in the afternoon. I sat down on an aluminum chair and seated the child, who hardly moved, opposite me. A woman of forty was sitting in the corner, and about every fifteen minutes her soul had a sudden contraction, and she'd scream loudly and mutter something in Ladino I didn't understand. Her back trembled. Who knows, I said to myself, maybe her son died of cancer.

I ordered whipped cream and old strawberries at a reduced price for myself and the child. He ate about three and fell asleep with his head on the table. I ate mine and his, and could easily have eaten more. I was bloated, I couldn't move. I opened a button on my pants, and thought, Oh Dolly, you're getting fatter by the day. You eat too much bread and yesterday's cakes that the cake-shops throw out. Your legs are like an elephant's already and your face is so huge that it frightens the child.

I gulped down a can of Schweppes and looked at the woman. My mood was in the pits. I'd just closed my exhibition and chucked everything into an enormous dumpster. The woman turned around and saw me, and it was evident that she was yearning to unburden her heart. Her face was sullen. She looked at the child and softened.

"What a darling," she said. "Where did you find him?"

"Just around the corner, a minute ago," I said. "You want him?"

"Are you selling?"

"If you're buying." I felt that I'd fallen into a trap. I looked at the child. Somehow I couldn't part from him like this. "So," I tried to change the subject, "what's your story? Why the tears?"

She sighed. "Is there a shortage of trouble in the world?"

"Don't get smart with me. What did your son die of, cancer? What kind of cancer did he have?"

"Cancer of the valleys."

"Oh my God, are you telling me that the valleys have got cancer too?"

"The valleys have got cancer, the fields have got cancer, the mountains, the rocks, everything."

"I see you've got cancer on the brain," I said, got up with my can of Schweppes, and sat down opposite her, smiling.

"My dear," she said to me, "the world's divided into two: those who've got cancer, and those who haven't got it."

"Which of them do you belong to?"

"Up to three weeks ago, to the ones who haven't, but now I'm riddled with metastases."

"Metastases! Oh my God!" I said.

"I feel like hanging myself."

I put out my hand and said: "Glad to meet you. I'm Professor Dolly, head of the oncology department at Kaplan Hospital, Rehovot. Would you like me to speed things up for you?"

"If you can."

I drew my pistol and shot one bullet, which went through her head and lodged in a landscape print behind her. I shook the kid awake and together we emerged into the dense fog of Dolly City. The fog of Dolly City—it envelops you like a silk gown, it pricks you like acupuncture, it goes straight to your nervous system.

It was April. In Dolly City, because of the eternal squabbling between Bureaucracy and Procedure, April drags on for three months, until it finishes saying everything it's got to say. I dragged myself along with the little one, who'd learned a long time ago that it didn't pay to mess with me.

In Dolly City the priests and nuns pop up out of nowhere, or maybe they come out of the walls, they crawl out from the cracks between the stones. I haven't got a clue, I don't know how it happens. The nuns and priests are dressed in black, and they're always running, you can always catch sight of the hems of their habits disappearing round the corner.

I sat on the curb and ate shit. The kid ate shit too. What more can I say? We finished off with cheesecake. I gave the kid a burned piece, I don't want him getting a sweet tooth, I can't afford dentists, and if there's one thing I don't know the first thing about, it's dentistry.

I looked at a priest running down the street after another priest, who was running after a nun, who was running after a black cat, who could tell where it all began and ended.

I remembered the Wailing Wall, that high wall with all the plants growing out of it, where people are always getting stabbed in the back if they try to reach it through the winding alleys, that towering wall that whenever I get anywhere near it—I'm told in eight languages to get back, to keep my distance, not to touch the sacred stones, not to desecrate the place with my impurity.

I wanted to send God a message, and taking a trip to the Wall was out of the question for numerous reasons. I sat and thought how I was going to get a message to God in his heaven if I was grounded in Dolly City? I realized I needed an intermediary. I spotted a priest or a nun and the kid and I ran after him-slash-her for three hours, over and under the botanical gardens, over and under bridges, but he-slash-she eluded us. In the afternoon we sat down on the steps of the Museum of Colonialism, resting from our barren pursuit.

I said to my son:

"Son, your mother has to find an intermediary who will take her words, fold them up, make them into an airplane, and send them flying into the great beyond."

The road to Kfar Habad, the Orthodox village, was full of radioactive fallout. All kinds of measuring instruments warned the travelers on the road against overexposure, and I, aggressively over-protective mother that I am, was filled with anxiety and instructed my son not to breathe. At least his lungs would not be contaminated.

Pan-T planes cruised above us like primordial birds, flying southeast or northwest or whatever direction their twinkling screens said they were flying in. British Airways planes cut across the yawning immensity of the sky too—but Pan-T is a whole other league. We were driving in a Beetle convertible I'd stolen back in town. I turned on the radio and listened to Gregorian chants.

Desert winds carrying mustard gas beat against the Beetle with tropical audacity. The child was tied down in the backseat with about five hundred belts. A sign saying Kfar Habad pointed left, and I turned obediently onto a road that wended its way through a dry creek.

People always look up with admiration to whatever is stronger than they are. Crazy people like saying that the craziness is stronger than them. Not me. I may be crazy, but it's not stronger than I am.

I penetrated the village in the afternoon. Men were standing under the trees and praying or dancing like dervishes, since the Hasidic shtick was, of course, *joie de vivre*—radioactive fallout or not.

I got out of the car, as fat as I was, a round, waddling ball, a balloon, a walking mountain with a checked cloth cap on my head and another on the head of my son. I approached one of the worshippers, who immediately said:

"It says in the Torah: Pour out thy fury upon the goyim that know thee not. Do you pour?"

"Do I pour out my fury? I don't think I've ever done anything but pour out my fury."

"Do you pour out your fury in any old direction, or do you hit the goyim?"

"Look, I'm dying to hit the goyim, really dying. And I've hit a few of them too, in Germany, in Düss—"

"Germany doesn't count," said the Hasid, who was long, long-limbed, long-faced, long-haired and long-bearded—black with flecks of gray.

"Why?" I asked.

"I'm taking care of Germany myself. It's being taken care of. You're wasting your time."

"So what's available?"

"You'll have to look at our lists."

The conversation broke up to smithereens. It began to snow and the fellow ran home, while I hurried back to the Beetle. My son was sitting inside shivering with cold, his lips as blue as the deep sea. I threw my coat over him and turned on the radio. It said that people today were moving from east to west, and that all movement from west to east had come to a complete halt. I imagined European tribes galloping on wild horses in Europe during the ninth or the seventh century, before all those barbarian hordes became so full of themselves, their asses grew to hippo-size scale, and they begun flooding the world with their dumb ideas.

I started the engine and drove slowly down the whitening paths of the village as it snowed and rained simultaneously. I was looking for their archives, to see the list and find an available goy kingdom. I wanted to know who else was taking care of the Germans, and if what I'd done in Stephanie Poldark's orphanage had been taken into account. I wanted to see who was taking care of pouring out his fury on the Brazilians, the Swedes, the Mongolians, who was screwing the neutral Swiss, with all their skiing and white snow, and all their ridiculous slalom competitions, which they watch in woolen hats and gloves, cheering from the sidelines.

I reached the archives, but they were closed because of the situation. It stopped snowing and raining. I got out, holding my son's icy hand, and looked for someone I could confide in so he could pass it on for me, right on to the top.

I looked at the wooden doors. I knew that behind most of them sat an elderly man with a long white beard and a twinkle in his eye, and indeed, when I opened a few doors carefully, and I and my son peeped in, that was exactly what we saw.

"Can I help?" said the Hasid revealed behind the door.

"Yes," I said quickly, "you can tell God that it was me who killed my father, not the cancer. That's to say, he was dying of cancer, but the lethal drug that killed him was injected into his IV by yours truly, mercy killing, yeah right. Can you pass that on to God?"

"Why don't you squirt it out to him yourself?" he said and returned to his perusal of the Talmud.

"You want a bullet in the head?" I said and took out my pistol.

But I didn't shatter his skull, I let him go on living, and the child and I went on living too.

We returned to the Beetle, but it was beginning to get on my nerves so I set it on fire to get a bit warm. I set out for the road with my son running after me shouting: "Wait for me, wait for me, wait for me." I kept looking behind my shoulder, not at him, but in the hope of getting a ride from some Hasid who had decided to abandon the faith of his fathers. But they all stuck to their old ideas and I was obliged to head back to town with a drooling hooligan of a truck driver. The kid laid his head on my shoulder, and I felt the hollows in his skull, a reminder of the bygone days when his head was at the head of my agenda. Although his touch freaked me out, I didn't hurl him to the other end of the cabin, but allowed his head to bounce up and down on my shoulder in accordance with the potholes and bumps in the road.

I examined myself. I wanted to see if I was still seeing cancer everywhere. I sensed that the road had cancer, this freeway, Route No. 1, was riddled with cancer, and so was the driver, but it all left me cold. I no longer felt the urge to open them up and take it out before it spread. I said to myself: Honey, just drop it.

That same day I figured out the way to fight my insanity: ignore it. I taught myself to treat my madness the way you treat a crazy person you meet on the street—you humor him, nod your head, and move on. "Move on"—these are the key words. Look and learn, I said to myself, a man goes out of his mind. He can leave it behind and move on. He can take that crazy mind of his and put it away, isolate it, and if possible tie it down—just as they do to crazy people themselves. For weeks I worked on this isolation, I isolated the thought that cancer had taken over the world, that cancer was the devil, that the devil had cancer.

The boy was six and a half, maybe more. I took him to Rosh Hanikra. I bought him a croissant and let my thoughts wander all afternoon. We sat on the cliff and watched the cable cars taking people down to the grotto to see the sea coming in and frothing and foaming precisely up to the points marked by the Nature Protection Society. In summer, the sea is too polite and tactful to make fools of the Nature Protectors in front of the tourists. Only in winter, when there's nobody there, it does what it likes and doesn't give a damn.

We went straight back to our den, to sleep, to forget, to get away from it all.

Months passed, like they always do, the show must go on and all that bullshit. People were deeply depressed, but no one wanted me to give them a massage or an enema, or even work with them on correct breathing.

We were down to our last crust, and we went to the only normal place left in Dolly City—the Carmel Market. It's unbelievable how organized everything is there! Rows of smiling stall-owners who know exactly what they're selling, their hands yellow with nicotine, all kinds of funguses sprouting on their necks. Lines of professional hawkers to the left and right, and in the middle, the moonlighters, yelling out warnings when a municipal inspector arrives.

We wandered down the streets of the market. With one hand I held my son, and in the other a wicker basket, which I filled with leftover fruit and vegetables and bits of chicken. We reached the stall that sold yellow antidepressants by the kilo, mountains of yellow pills. The hawker ladled them with a big spoon into brown paper bags, and people bought them like peanuts.

I bought two kilos of pills to last me the month, and swallowed eight at once. I let the kid have a couple as well, to get him into the swing of things.

At the market's exit I sat down on a bench and cracked pistachio nuts. Mothers with children hanging on their chests or backs, or still inside their stomachs, hurried past me, rushing from the Carmel Market to the black market on Lillenblum Street, where men in checked pants stand, their little pricks tucked into white y-fronts and their faces erased, as if someone had flattened them with a brick. They've all got $-shaped, crooked mouths from all the times they've hissed the black market rate of the dollar out of the corner of their mouths.

The kid looked at those children who had questionable fathers and fucked-up mothers, and I told him to thank me, to have a good look at these people worse off than me and be grateful that he'd fallen into my hands and not those of the really crazy women, the quiet ones who never say anything at all until they take a glass and smash it on their children's heads. And the kid, who thought that he'd finally found a chink in my armor, asked me for a popsicle shaped like a rooster. He'd gone too far. I seized his head firmly between my hands, gave him a good shake, and yelled if he'd like me to send him to a kibbutz in some valley. I told him that if he didn't shut up, I was going to send him to Beit Netofa Valley, to Kibbutz Ein Shemer, to the giant swings between the Poinciana trees.

The kid gave me a frightening look, a really frightening look, and I shut up, with a completely new anxiety rising in my breast. I shivered at the thought that I'd made him mentally ill, that I was beginning to pay the price for his carved-up childhood. My blood ran cold at the thought that from now on he was going to wear out the rest of his days in lunatic asylums. I could already see him at the age of sixty, sitting on a bench with a look of incurable insanity in his eyes, his hair uncombed and thinning. This abyss pulled me down like chewing gum. Instead of facing it, I went to sleep and dreamed that he was fucking me, my own child was fucking me. When I woke up I must have looked like Charlotte Rampling after a lay.

As for my son, he was standing in front of me, clean and neat, all dressed up in new clothes—I think he was even wearing a checked flannel waistcoat—hanging onto the hand of my only sister, whom I hadn't seen for years.

"Natasha," I said, my head spinning. "What are you doing in Dolly City? Have you gone out of your mind?"

"I'm opening a shelter for battered children, sister. Children of perverted, dangerous parents, sister. I'm taking the child away from you, I'm confiscating him. You know why."

"And when are you going to return him to me? After all he's my child, for better or for worse—"

"When you return to the '67 borders," she retorted.

"What?"

"You heard me," and she grabbed the kid and marched off in the direction of Allenby Street, and he walked calmly next to her without so much as a backward glance.

Rain in Dolly City isn't just bullshit, it comes down as thick as spaghetti, but for five years it hasn't rained a drop. Friendly missiles were fired from the outskirts of the city to tear the virgin clouds wide open and get things moving, but the missiles entered the clouds and got stuck inside them like horses' dicks.

To overcome their depression, the inhabitants of Dolly City swallowed yellow pills in increasing quantities. I too was plunged in gloom, and I too increased my dosage.

I earned my living exclusively from enemas, I became a real expert in the field. A certain accountant I serviced told me that for several nights he had dreamed that the numbers themselves were pursuing him, intent on fucking him up the ass, and he didn't know what to do. He wasn't the only one in Dolly City to have this dream. My clients—a cross section of the demented population suffering from a representative collection of deprivations—would pour out their boring confessions to me, so boring that even my hair went to sleep. When people start talking, it's like that trick Itzik the magician used to do in our skyscraper, the one when you take a yellow handkerchief out of your mouth, and then a red one, a green one and a purple one, and so forth and so on, there's just no end to it.

I was growing old. I turned forty-one. I got even fatter. All I ate was chunks of halva. I think I weighed around ninety kilos, and that's without the child. Frost descended on the city, there was no escaping it. The colder it grew the more halva I devoured. I was crazy about halva, halva's really something.

The telephone poles shivered with cold, birds froze in mid-flight and fell like stones. The sculptors went completely crazy. Everything that petrified from the cold—they claimed as their own work. Minor wars broke out among the sculptors, quarrels in broad daylight, public disputes on street corners.

I joined the down-and-outs round their crackling fires. People said nothing and tried to get warm. There was no smoke without twenty people standing round it. They breathed in the vapors coming out of each other's mouths, and so, despite their revulsion, people stuck together.

Another April came to an end, the fifth in succession, and February arrived. The sky was overcast, not with clouds but with planes— Migs and Mirages of the French Air Force, dropping bombs on my only grazing ground. For several months their planes had been bombing Dolly City for no apparent reason. They would simply appear in the sky two or three times a month, shit on us, and fly away again. I ran with everybody else to the botanical gardens for shelter, because people said that the French would never touch the botanical gardens—they were sentimental about plants on account of their big perfume industry. But this was bullshit. The botanical gardens were thoroughly bombed, and I really had to laugh when I saw the gigantic tropical flowers with unexploded bombs stuck in their jaws.

I was deeply depressed. For years I'd been preparing for a cancer attack, for years I'd been identifying cancer cells wherever I looked—and along came the French Air Force with a few of their asshole pilots, dropping booby-trapped ostrich eggs all over my moon.

One day, let's say in March, the twenty-second of March, or maybe the thirtieth of December—only you, God, know what's happened to my memory—two Concords collided over Dolly City with a mighty crash. I lay on a bench and watched all the people and their parts falling down. The rescue teams prevented the crowds from turning the survivors into kebabs.

But the people of Dolly City had never in their lives taken any notice of anyone's pleas, and they went ahead and did what they did.

I was hungry as well. I was really dying to get my teeth into something, say a chocolate croissant, but the bakeries were shut, the people wanted to eat meat. I went into the graveyard of the French soldiers who'd fallen in World War I. Pale crosses with all kinds of Jean-Clauds and Jean-Pauls. I lay down on the charged earth and took a nap.

I opened and closed my eyes. I knew I had to get up—people have to get up, they have to stand on their own two feet! And if they don't want to—too bad. They must get up!

I got up and stood on my feet and felt dizzy. I could hardly straighten my back, my vertebrae hurt. I went back to town. People were walking in the streets, they were drinking beer in bars, they were fucking behind curtains. I went into a café, I asked for a glass of water and swallowed eighteen pills all at once, to give me a little lift. But it didn't have any effect. Those things are useless. I walked down the street until I found a bib with a picture of Donald Duck hanging from a power line. I found myself climbing up the pole— I took the risk for that bit of cloth. I rescued the bib, I examined it, it looked more or less okay to me, and I set out for the home established by my sister, the social worker—a shelter for battered children and debilitated old folks.

"What's that?" asked my sister, whose hair had turned a little gray.

"A bib."

"Who for?"

"The kid." I recoiled. Why did she ask who for? "Are you trying to tell me that he's dead?"

"No."

"So where is he?"

"In the pool."

"What pool, you have a pool?"

"There's a little lake inside the volcano." She cast a glance at the bib. "That's too small for him," she said.

"Too small?"

"The child's thirteen years old, Dolly. How dumb are you? You think that if you haven't seen him for six years, he's stayed the same as the last time you saw him?"

She went inside, and I followed her. Her curls were tied back with a black ribbon. She'd grown thinner, she looked like a stick.

A group of merry adolescents passed us. I tried to look for the kid among them but he wasn't there. I found him in the pool, lying in a black rubber tube. My sister turned on her heel and walked away.

I looked at this creature inside the tube, and I couldn't communicate with him, I couldn't find the words. I couldn't even say hello. There was too much history. I said to myself, this is it, Dolly. The monster you created in your madness. Be prepared for the worst, I said to myself, but I knew that there were no limits to reality's imagination, no limits at all.

The boy let his head fall back with a blissful expression and wet his long, black, curly hair. Although he looked familiar, I wondered if it was him at all. I had one way of making sure.

"Get out of the water, that's an order!" I shouted.

He snickered, but nevertheless he obeyed, jumped out of the tube, and swam to the ladder. When he got out of the water and came toward me, I noticed that his stomach was scarred, but anyone's stomach could be scarred.

"Turn around," I said.

He obeyed, and I saw the map of the Land of Israel on his back. The map was amazingly accurate and up-to-date; someone had gone over all the lines and expanded them as the child had grown. I examined the map carefully, and one thing stood out:

He had returned to the '67 borders! Beyond belief!

Yes, that's the generation gap for you, I reflected. My mother spits on the Arabs, I look them straight in the eye, and one day my son will lick their assholes.

The kid went to get dressed, and I waited for him impatiently outside the showers. Things change. I grow fat or thin, swell up or shrink, and my son grows tall, and looks down his nose at me.

He came out to meet me, neatly combed and wearing jeans and a colorful T-shirt—elegantly dressed, in comparison to the rags worn by the inhabitants of Dolly City, clothes without rhyme or reason.

"Shall we go?" he said.

"Where to?" I asked him.

He didn't answer, but began walking towards the gym, where boys and girls two or three years older or younger than him were exercising. Twelve-year-old girls were walking on bars, and other kids were doing corkscrew somersaults in the air. An impressive setup, this place my sister's built, I said to myself as we left.

We emerged in the street. Although it was only a quarter of an hour, maybe half an hour, since I'd entered the institute, it seemed to me that five years had passed. The air seemed different, I myself seemed different, the streets seemed to have broadened, the buildings to be a little further apart, and here and there I even saw a few flags, but I couldn't tell which countries they belonged to. From what I could see when I looked up—the sun was shining behind the buildings, the sky was above me, even the moon was stuck up there in its usual rut. I looked at my son, at his profile. I said to myself, his profile, I never touched his profile, that's why he's got a profile.

My son talked and talked, as if he'd swallowed a radio. He met people, people shook his hand, he slapped them on the shoulder, he stopped to exchange a few sentences with them about some rock concert, I wasn't really listening. I was busy realizing myself. We kept walking aimlessly, or so I thought, but after a while it turned out that he was leading me to a barbershop. He asked the barber to trim his black curls.

"Wouldn't that be a real shame?" I asked him, but again he didn't answer me.

I sat down behind him and looked at his hair falling to the floor. There was a woman there having her hair set with rollers, and another one with bits of silver foil stuck onto her hair, whose face looked quite frightening. The assistant barbers moved about, dancing around the head barber who was busy joking about the political situation with my son, who displayed surprising curiosity and even more surprising expertise. He knew all about the regional conflicts, he understood all about the interests of the surrounding states, he even understood the motives of the more distant ones, and argued with the barber about Churchill and Chamberlain and many other people whose names begin with Ch, like Che Guevara. I looked into the distance, at the mountains in the large landscape painting on the far wall of the barbershop. I asked myself when was it coming, in other words, when was he going to ask me about all those scars, and from what diseases exactly he'd suffered and was currently suffering. I dreaded this moment because I was already worn out by all that medicine and disease. I didn't want to hear another word about it.

Half an hour after we'd returned to the street and I'd bought him a cheeseburger in a pita, he told me that he wanted to undergo psychoanalysis, that he felt he had something to get out of his system.

"Who put that into your head, my sister?" I asked sourly. "It sounds like her style. Just because she used to be in the business she thinks . . ."

"Everyone at the home undergoes psychoanalysis," said the boy. "Straight after their bar mitzvah—psychoanalysis. It's the rule."

I put my hands on my hips: "And who do you think is going to pay for your psychoanalysis?" I asked provocatively. "Your father's bank perhaps?"

"Whoever's paying for my bar mitzvah will pay for my psycho-analysis."

"You—you—you—watch out, mister," I warned him. "You don't know who you're messing with! You watch out for me!" I waved my finger in the air.

"But why, Mom?" he said with a sly smile. "What's wrong with it? I'm having a bar mitzvah under the open sky in the national park, and after that everyone's going to the Safari."

"The Safari? Are you crazy? You want to take people to the Safari? Who do you think is going to pay for it? What's the matter with you, you think I've got a gold-mine? Who do you think is going to buy tickets for you and your guests to go to the Safari?"

"Whoever's going to pay for my psychoanalysis."

"And who is going to pay for your psychoanalysis?"

"Pan-T."

"What did you say?"

"You heard me, Pan-T."

"The Israeli National Airline?"

"Yes. They pay for all the activities of all the kids at the home. Your sister, my aunt," he giggled, "obtained ten years' funding from them. She raises the kids, and the ones she recommends undergo aptitude tests to see if they're fit to work for Pan-T."

"I can't believe what I'm hearing here!" I cried, and looked at those double-decker buses. "I can't believe what I'm hearing," I muttered again, and I thought to myself that even in this realized existence, you're never free of anything. In the elevator to hell I'd bump into the first man I ever slept with.

My son and I walked a long distance in silence. He strode half a meter in front of me, and I trailed behind him. Both of us were deep in thought. Mine could be described as coils of barbed wire, or abandoned tumbleweed.

"You know," I cried eventually, "psychoanalysis, what do you need psychoanalysis for? Ignore your past. Just don't take any notice of it. All those childhood complexes, those pacifiers and daddy's underpants, what good can they do you now?"

"Forget it, Mom. I'm going for it," he said without even turning round to look at me. "Daniella," he continued, "the Pan-T social worker, studied social work with your sister at Bar Ilan University, and they're both terrific."

The boy went on talking, but I've got a low attention threshold, and I stopped trying to understand what he was getting at.

A few minutes later I was flooded by the memory of that last harassment of my weary mind, and I addressed the boy firmly:

"I forbid you unequivocally to have any contact whatsoever with the national airline company! I'm telling you right now that if you go into psychoanalysis you're no son of mine. Is that understood?!" I shrieked.

The boy's eyes filled with tears. He gave me a wounded look, turned away, and began to run. As soon as he reached the corner it began to pour with rain, ah yes, Dolly City finally got a cold shower. I charged after him, but he eluded me, and I sat down on a trash can in an alley, wet to the marrow of my bones, took out a handkerchief and wiped my face.

Throughout the following hours I searched. I called out to the boy, I stood on the trash cans and shouted: "Son, you son of a bitch, answer me!"

I walked between the buildings, some of them hit by the French bombs. I was a bundle of regrets. In an instant I'd given up my demand that he refrain from getting analyzed. I said to myself, why not, let him do it, let him bring up the memory of my morbid operations, let him know what he's up against, let him understand that his mother wanted to be responsible for him in the fullest sense of the word, and not to share the responsibility with anyone else, including Creation, or all its synonyms put together.

I understood that I'd been wrong, that I should have let things happen. I mean, the child was thirteen years old, and he was still alive. Technically speaking, there was no need for all that poking and prodding. I had carved him up for nothing. I wandered on, in terrible despair. I tried to pick up radar signals, like a mother-bat, but it was a no-go.

"God help me," I murmured, and sat down on a bench under a heavy rain shower. Thunder and lightning struck, and suddenly a man stood before me wearing a black raincoat and hat and carrying a black umbrella. He smiled a pale smile at me. His lips were almost white. I had no doubt that he was fatally ill. When I looked harder, I saw that he was McMillan from *McMillan & Wife*, but something wasn't kosher. I assumed that he was just another of Dolly City's imposters, another one of the delusional lunatics.

"Pleased to meet you," he said and held out his hand. "I work for Hercule Poirot, my name is McMillan."

"Pleased to meet you," I said with suspicion. "I'm Professor Dolly, head of the geriatric department in the Beilinson Hospital, Petah Tikvah."

We shook hands. His hand was frozen.

I immediately suspected that the man was connected to Pan-T, because my father, instead of actually paying attention to people around him, the minute he came home from work would begin to read French pocket books starring Hercule Poirot and other such characters. These were books with large print and photographs of revolvers on their shiny, creased covers. He would plough through eight or nine of them in a week.

McMillan suggested that I phone the police about my son and report him as a missing person. A real wiseass—all the pay phones in Dolly City have been out of order for years. The minute you pick up the receiver you hear a busy signal. It's impossible to phone anywhere except Yavne, and in Yavne they pick up the phone and ask if they can help you, but it's only a recording.

McMillan spread a map of Dolly City on the muddy pavement, and for the first time in my life, I looked down on things from above. What can I say about the things I looked down on?

I accorded them all due respect. McMillan pointed to the Wells of Despair, the Lakes of Fear, the Swamps of Boredom, and the Canyons of Mannerism, and all those arrows signifying people's migration patterns.

He said that he thought he'd go and look for my son at the Trappist Monastery—maybe one of those taciturn monks would open his trap. The guy sounded like a total imbecile to me, and I soon realized that it was all total nonsense. I ignored him, and after a series of sentences that received no acknowledgement, he said:

"One day you'll be sorry. You'll pay for having insulted me!"

"Aha," I snorted, "I'm shaking in my boots."

"You think you're so clever—your father is dead. If he were alive you wouldn't dare."

"Oh yeah? How do you know?"

"It's not so hard to know."

"You know what? You're disgusting, you make me sick," I flared up. "I'm gonna smash your face in, so fuck off! I'll tear your brains to strips of crumpled cellophane."

"Shh, shh," said McMillan, patting my shoulder to calm me down. "Shh, you're going to be all right."

"Kiss my ass," I said and pushed him.

"If your father were alive—you wouldn't dare talk like that. With him around you'd never have dared say the word ass."

"Who says?"

"Nobody."

"Shh, shh, shh-ut up," I said. "And kiss my ass."

"Why don't you freshen up your vocabulary a bit, Dolly?"

"Kiss it," I said.

He walked away, and I boiled over with rage. I shrieked like some bleeding heart samurai. I shot him in the back, and he fell bleeding to the ground and lay there dying for quite a while. All that time he twitched and moaned, but I did nothing about it. After he died, I came closer and rummaged through his pockets. I found my father's big bunch of keys with all the keys to his secret drawers in the Pan-T offices and at home. I put them in my pocket and walked off, but instead of the sense of reality, of having been realized, I felt the burning pain of loss, then a black cloak covered me, and I struggled in vain inside it like a tigress caught in a trap.

Once more I was in the loony bin, tied down to the bed and listening to a lecture delivered by one of the lunatics, while all the others listened to him attentively. I understood that he believed he was running for election to the Knesset, and he was asking all the loonies to join him and get their families' signatures on various forms he had prepared from litmus paper, or something of the sort. The lunatics suggested things he should add to his party platform, and he shared his doubts with them. One of the items on his platform—as I understood it—was that the state should pay for the psychiatric treatment of its citizens, since the state was responsible for unbalancing their minds.

Someone wrote on the wall, Madness is a ripe orange, and therefore it should be wrapped up and sent to Europe in crates stamped with the word Jaffa.

My son walked into the room, with an open book under his arm. He smiled at me, and said: "How do you feel today, Mom? Better?" And he put his hand on my forehead.

My head was heavy, I didn't know what they'd fed me. I looked around to see if my environment was still cancerous, but I couldn't even glimpse a common cold. Someone had obviously plucked my ripe orange, I thought, and was horrified to feel a very sharp stab of sorrow. I realized that they'd done something to me, but since my hands were tied I couldn't touch myself, to see if they had opened me up.

My son read my thoughts.

"Sorry, Mom," he said.

My lips were dry. I licked them.

"Water," I said.

"Sorry, Mom, you're not allowed water. Only tea with sugar." And he put a blue plastic cup of dark tea to my lips. I opened my mouth slightly and sucked up the drink. With the boy's help I drank up the whole cup, and leaned back, fixing my eyes on a bit of white curtain.

"Tell me something," I said to my son.

"What?"

"Where were you? Where did you disappear to?"

"I was at B.G. Airport," grinned the boy. "I've begun dialysis."

"Dialysis?" I got the word out with difficulty. "Weren't we talking about psychoanalysis? Don't you want to have psychoanalysis any more? Are you content with dialysis?"

"I'm content with dialysis," he said and gave me a mischievous wink. "I've decided to look ahead, and to forget all the bullshit."

"What do you mean?"

"You know what I mean. I mean that you might be said to be the only mother in the world who knows her son inside out."

"Ah," I shuddered.

"Yes," he said and laid the book on my mattress.

"What are you reading?" I asked.

Magellan's Voyage, he said in a satisfied tone.

"What? Good." I whispered, and he didn't answer, only a diligent glint flashed in his eyes. I was too weak to say a word. I closed my eyes and almost in a dream I heard my son saying:

"Guess what?"

"What?" I opened my eyes.

"I'm joining the army. They've accepted me!"

"What?"

"I'm joining the army."

"At your age?"

"They accepted me. Yes," he lifted his chin proudly.

"The air force?" I was terrified.

"No," he said. "The navy."

"The navy?"

"Yes, the navy cadet school. The Academy of Brutal Seamanship. Don't try to stop me. Give me your blessing. Believe me, Mom," he said with sparkling eyes, "to sail, Mom, to sail with all those white sails, in the wind, to get out of Dolly City, to sail to Sierra Leone, to see the natives jumping on the shore, to go round Africa in seventy days. To all those wonderful places that only the great explorers experienced. I've decided, Mom, I'm giving everything I've got to the sea."

"And who's paying?"

"Pan-T. The idea behind it, I think, is for me to discover new places for Pan-T to fly to."

"Come on, do you really think I buy any of that?"

"Buy what?"

"I . . . I . . . I . . ." I said and noticed my new difficulty in speaking.

"Ciao," he said.

He ran out of the ward, rang the bell, the armored door opened, and for a split second a few sunbeams filtered in.

A redheaded, curly-haired psychiatrist of about forty walked into the room, her face exuding the bitterness of a woman with no options—there are things in life that have to be done, so why shouldn't she be the one to do them? She was wearing a white cotton dress and over it a white gown. I knew her, she was treating me, God only knows what I'd already told her.

"How are you, doctor?" she said.

"I could ask you the same question."

"I'm well, thank you. There were a few traffic jams on the way. I don't know how they can call that road a highway."

"Doctor," I said.

"Yes."

"I understand that these people are your patients," I nodded towards the political meeting that was taking place not far from us. "But my case is different. Even if I am crazy—I'm not like them. I'm special, if only because of the fact that I'm a doctor myself."

"Yes," she said.

"My heart aches," I said.

"Mine too, believe me. When I see all those dead people on the roads, when I read the newspaper—my heart aches."

"But my heart really aches. I've got pains on the left side of my chest and in my right arm."

"It's stress, Dolly. It's nothing. It's the field of thorns after the fire. Now we have to wait patiently for new seeds to sprout."

"What new seeds?" I remembered Gordon. "I was happy. I was realizing myself. I had a goal. What have you done to me? Why did you clean the metastases out of my eyes?"

"We didn't clean anything out of them, you simply came to your senses! Look at me—have I got cancer?"

"Maybe," I said but I wasn't upset. Previously, the mere possibility would have freaked me out. Now I said, "Only a CT will tell."

"You know," she said, "this is the first time in years that I feel I'm making progress. Working with you is a real treat. You're quite reasonable in comparison to other crazy people, it's a pleasure to work with you."

"Thank you," I said.

"Now you'll feel longing for your child. It's natural, do you understand me? When I tell you that it's natural, don't resist it. Go with it, Dolly. Perhaps he'll send you photos, and you'll put them in your wallet in the transparent compartment, where your father put the photo of you aged four next to the Eiffel Tower."

"How do you know about that photo?"

"You told me," she said. "You told me a lot of things. It was really nice. It's okay to enjoy life a little. It's okay."

"What?"

I massaged my throbbing temples. The doctor patted my shoulder affectionately and went on to say: "You have to remember—your child may die in battle. He may die in battle, you've got to get that into your head. He may die of drowning, or a shark may kill him, if he fell overboard. You have to get it into your head that he may even die of cancer, but it's reasonable to assume that if he dies soon, it will be in battle. Because severe battles are being waged in the ocean. Very severe indeed. They say those French sons of bitches are going for broke." She paused for a moment and then continued: "And then, if he dies in battle, you'll be a bereaved mother, just as if you die he'd be an orphan. There are names for things! There are identities! For God's sake, Dolly," she cried, "take the lifeline I'm holding out to you, take it and let's put an end to this! Don't you understand? Why? Why? Tell me, are you still convinced that you're a doctor who studied in Katmandu?"

"Of course," I said.

"So where's your passport?"

"What?"

"Where's your passport? Where's the stamp in your passport saying that you were in the Far East? We've bent over backwards trying to find it. Your mother says that your sister's got it, and your sister says that you've got it yourself."

"I don't know where my passport is," I muttered. "Seriously, I don't know. I don't know exactly what you want of me either. I've told you twenty times that I'm a doctor. That I studied medicine in Katmandu. I keep on telling people all the time, and they believe me—so why don't you? Do you think that you're better than everyone else? More talented? I simply don't understand what makes you people tick. What makes you tick? Why do you keep smiling? What makes you laugh?"

"What makes me laugh?" she asked.

"Yes."

"Mainly improvisations. All kind of skits in the street, at four o'clock in the afternoon. And sunbathing naked on the roof. Those are amusing things."

"I think I can confidently say that you're completely normal," I said. She looked desperate. Her mind wandered round the ward— she was looking for a new, fresh, convincing argument. And then her eyes fell on a new inmate called Kobi. This fellow was completely nuts, he was brilliant, he had a T-shirt that said: I'm a mad genius. I could read the psychiatrist's thoughts. She averted her eyes from him and turned to face me, slightly parting her lips, which were smeared with poppy-red lipstick.

"Don't say it, I know," I said.

"If you know, then what do you say?"

"What do I say?"

"You want to be like him? He's a hopeless case. I'm violating my professional ethics and telling you that he's finished, there's no hope for him."

"I don't know."

"Do yourself a favor, Dolly, Doctor Dolly. Enough with the bullshit already. Enough, okay?"

PART
FOUR

I went out to the ploughed streets of Dolly City, to the indifferent streets, to the fountains pissing in an arc. I pulled down my pants and peed into the fountain, I spilled out whatever I had and made my contribution to the art of sculpture. When I was finished, I looked at the statue of the little boy. It was a boy of about four years old hugging a tree trunk. I touched the statue with my soft fingertips. Then I felt better and turned in the direction of the main post office on Allenby Street, where I found a letter sent by my son from his marine-combat academy.

Like his other letters, this one was a short missive of five lines at the most. He wrote that the Pacific Ocean, like a lot of other myths, was not pacific at all, but stormy, and the water was red with all the battles being fought there. Every two minutes they saw a booby-trapped dolphin, and schools of hungry sharks were chasing their ships. When it came to waging war, the French knew no bounds, just as they knew no bounds when it came to cooking themselves a good meal.

The boy was thrilled by the whole affair, it had completely gone to his head. He told me about all the different weapons. His letters suffered from a piratical incoherence, he jumped from subject to subject, his handwriting was sloppy, but at the same time as clear as daylight. It was often difficult to decipher his letters because some of them were stained with blood. He wrote to me on Pan-T notepaper, and this killed me. I racked my brains: what was the national airline's real interest in teaching my son selected passages of battleship doctrine and brutal seamanship? What, in the name of all the years my father had devoted to the company, were they looking for in the sea? And why had they chosen my son? Why?

I didn't believe they really wanted him to find them new destinations to fly to. Pan-T was full of workers who were dying for the chance to go abroad at the company's expense. Workers much more qualified than my sister's soldiers, who with all due respect, however battered they were, had never eaten chicken, rice, and carrots at the Pan-T canteen. They had never shown their name tags to the guard when they entered the company offices at the Ben Gurion Airport. They didn't even have name tags.

I couldn't phone Pan-T and ask them right out what they wanted with my son because all the public phones in Dolly City were out of order, apart from which I didn't have a phone token. Phone tokens in Dolly City are rare, and there are people who are prepared to kill for one, on the chance that one fine day the phone booths might be fixed once and for all, and they would finally be able to make a single direct call.

I decided to beg for money. I thought that maybe someone would throw me a token by mistake, but in vain. Pennies and gobs of pustular spit were all I got for my pains. I realized that if I wanted a phone token, I would have to steal it. I picked the pockets of passersby left and right, but none of them had a token. Their pockets were full of used bus tickets and punched train coupons, but nothing else. I could, ostensibly, have gone to the Pan-T building on Ben Yehuda Street, or driven to the airport, banged on tables, done my own version of the Intifada, and demanded that somebody tell me what was going on here—but I wasn't cut out for it. I could only do it by telephone, with twenty handkerchiefs to disguise my voice, and the option of disconnecting at any moment.

One day I read a short item in the newspaper to the effect that there were a lot of phone tokens in the women's prison. The prisoners threaded them onto nylon strings and the prison authorities sent them to all kinds of international congresses, as if they were traditional works of art made by ancient Assyrian women, so and so years ago.

I went to the railway station, collected my instruments from my locker, and took an express streetcar to the Neve-Tirza prison. They put me in a glass cell and left me there for ten minutes while they ran all kinds of security tests on me, which reminded me vividly of that time I went to the Pan-T offices in Paris and asked them to move my flight back a few days.

When they'd finished with me, a buzzer sounded, and a warden, who actually seemed like a nice lady, came up to me in her uniform and asked me what I wanted. I said that I was a gynecologist, and I'd come to assist one of the prisoners give birth. I assumed that the statistical odds were overwhelmingly in favor of one of the prisoners or female wardens being in labor at that moment. In Dolly City female prisoners get mysteriously pregnant without leaving the prison walls, and nobody knows who knocked them up. I once read somewhere that it was the female wardens themselves who got the prisoners pregnant, but it never said how.

The nice warden led me into the prison and told me that all the women were doing time because they'd murdered their children, either through criminal neglect, insanity, or cold-blooded stoicism. From the way she spoke it appeared that child-murder in Dolly City was folklore, and she went on to ask me if I too had murdered my children, but I didn't answer her. She inquired on tactfully, asking if any such thought had ever crossed my mind, and I nodded.

The eyes of the little murderesses stared at me as I passed them with my bag in my hand. Some of them swore at me, one of them begged me to give her an abortion. On principle, I wouldn't have minded, but the warden told me that she wasn't even pregnant, she was simply addicted to the anesthetic from all the abortions she had in the past.

On a disgusting bed in a stinking room, one leg here and one leg there, lay the prisoner. She cursed her mother and her father for copulating and bringing her into the world.

Things moved fast, and twelve hours later she gave birth to a son with his umbilical cord coiled round his neck. I wanted to release him, but his mother begged me to let him suffocate in peace, she'd already been sentenced to life anyway for murdering her six children.

The child changed color, and departed this world as he had come into it.

I sewed the lady up and casually asked the warden:

"Have you got a phone token?"

"A phone token?"

"You want a token?" I heard a male voice behind me. I turned round and saw a hermaphrodite.

"Yes," I said.

"Where do you want to phone to?" inquired the warden who'd led me to the woman in labor.

"Out of town."

"Quickly, okay?"

"Okay."

I shall never forget the echo of her footsteps in the dim corridors of the prison. I looked right and left and said to myself, pay attention, Dolly, there's always someone deeper in shit, so shut up and be grateful that you're free to walk the streets instead of rotting here like this gang of lesbians. Suddenly the warden opened her mouth and gave out a few random bits of information, but I had no idea what to do with them. For example, she said that the prison wardens, including herself, were the daughters of old prisoners who'd managed to survive.

We went into the prison directress's office. The walls were lined with monitors, incubators containing premature babies, and glass jars in which fetuses floated in formalin, just as I'd seen thirty-five years earlier in the Museum of Human Anatomy in Ramat-Gan.

On a black, peeling desk stood two horses of dull gold, rearing up on their hind legs in a dueling position, their forelegs locked. Next to them a black telephone, dating back from the sixties, stood silently.

"Hurry up," my friend the warden urged me, "any minute now the directress will be coming out of the Jacuzzi with a white towel on her head and a white towel round her body."

I dialed the number which was so deeply etched in my memory, and the switchboard operator answered: "Pan-T at your service, good afternoon."

I didn't open my mouth.

"Pan-T at your service, good afternoon."

I put the receiver down on its cradle.

"Is there something wrong?" asked the warden.

Suddenly the prison directress emerged from the Jacuzzi with her two towels, just as my friend had warned me. She looked at me curiously.

"I'm looking for my roots," I said quickly, "I mean, the roots of my child. It's very probable that there's a certain pilot whose daughter is my child's real mother. The one who studied medicine at the Technion. I haven't managed to verify that yet, I've been trying for thirteen years," I said.

The directress let her towel drop to the floor, and hurriedly wrapped herself in a kimono.

"Sit down," she said and indicated the rusty chair opposite her, and she sat down herself, her hair dripping.

"Most of my prisoners," she said and wrung her hair, "are sure that their children aren't theirs. That's how they justify their murders. We work on them for years until they admit that they murdered their own children, and for years after that to convince them that it had nothing to do with mercy. Their guilt is really something else. The interesting thing is," she stuck a menthol cigarette in her mouth and lit it, for a moment losing track of what she was saying, "what's interesting is that even the women who perform abortions on themselves with knitting-needles are sure that it wasn't theirs. Before they leave the prison—if they ever do—I send my prisoners to psychological treatment, to see if there are any dark corners left that need sweeping out. Everyone, in my humble opinion, before any turning point in his life, if he leaves a town, or a village, or a neighborhood, or a prison, or anything else, should examine himself thoroughly to see if he hasn't got a few cobwebs somewhere, covering up a dirty secret code."

She combed her hair, and braided it in a Japanese plait. Then she began putting on makeup, and I asked myself who she was dolling herself up for like this, who was going to fuck her tonight.

"Even if the child is mine," I said, "it doesn't solve the problem of who in Pan-T is pulling strings and why."

"But it's one step forward." She stubbed out the half smoked cigarette in an ashtray. "Would you like me to find out for you?"

"Why should you do me such a service?"

"For no reason, I imagine. I do such things for fun, I like helping my fellow men to rehabilitate themselves. It's my pleasure."

"Do you have connections in Pan-T?"

"My stepmother, Roberta, works for the income tax authorities."

"So?"

"She knows people from all the companies in the country."

She made a series of phone calls but to no avail. In the meantime I drank coffee with sour milk, and eventually she apologized a thousand times and said that she felt she had misled me, that it made her feel terrible, and that she was going to give me two phone tokens, and hoped that I would forgive her for all the distress she had caused me. After I'd already gone, she called out and wished me good luck.

I walked the streets of Dolly City for a few hours, I ate eight grade F croissants, and sixty grade D wafers, and I was still hungry. I was dying for something sweet. I walked aimlessly, I didn't know what to do with myself. The thirteen public phones I passed were all out of order, and the exact phrasing of the question I was supposed to ask Pan-T grew increasingly hazy in my mind. I knew that there was no point in my opening my mouth until I had things a bit more in focus.

Suddenly I saw my sister, the social worker, walking down the street with a train of battered children trailing behind her. From a distance I noticed her agitation. My little sister was amazingly like my father—despair oozed from their every step, like wax dripping from a candle.

She recognized me and quickened her pace, she had bad news clearly written on her face. The closer she came to me, the worse the catastrophe grew. Her whole face twitched convulsively, and as we reached each other my heart pounded ferociously.

"What . . . what . . . what's wrong? Where's my child?"

"He's fine. It's Mother." She wiped away a tear.

"Dead?"

"Yes."

"Really?"

"Do you think I'd make up a thing like that?"

"Have you buried her?"

She sighed.

"Don't we all bury our parents? We ourselves grind them into dust! Children kill their parents, and the parents, in exchange, beat them bloody."

She stroked a battered child with cigarette scars and an iron-shaped burn across his face.

"Where have you been?" she said in a different tone and narrowed her eyes to white slits. "Your son wrote to me and said that you don't answer his letters. And our mother, poor thing, was looking for you. She wanted you to go and have an electrocardiogram. She was hysterical, she thought there was something wrong with your heart. Is it so hard for you to get hold of a phone token?"

I clutched the two phone tokens in my hand and kept quiet. I assumed that my sister had opened our mother's will. She'd probably left half her property to my son, when he turned eighteen, on condition that he didn't, on any account, live in Dolly City, but only in Tel Aviv, in north Tel Aviv, nowhere south of Bugrashov Street at least, otherwise he wouldn't get a penny. The other half she donated to my sister's shelter.

My sister had a sealed airmail envelope in her hand.

I grabbed the envelope. It said "to be opened after my death." She was dead, so I opened it, and found an open check made out to Pan-T.

"Oh my God," I said.

In the letter attached to the check she wrote in French that for years she'd known that the Pan-T airline company was plotting against me, but she couldn't say anything, because she didn't have enough money. Now that she'd died and donated her body to science (Oh my God, she'd donated her body to science!), she was ready to donate some of her money so that I could pay Pan-T back for all those free flights I'd taken when my father was alive. As long as the debt was still standing, she wrote, the company would go on persecuting me, and they'd never let me be. She concluded her letter with a bundle of abusive insults for a certain accountant who'd confronted my father once in their apartment building's stairwell, and instructed me again to add up all the times that I and the rest of the family had traveled abroad at the expense of the airline, as part of the benefits bestowed upon company employees and their families, add interest in arrears, and write the sum on the check.

I didn't have the least desire to return the money, but my mother was no longer alive for me to argue with her.

I managed to find a functioning telephone, and with my precious token I called one of the top directors of Pan-T and asked him straight out to what extent the company was involved in my son's naval training, and what their real interest was in making him a seaman.

He asked to me wait and accessed my son's personal file on the Pan-T database. Yes, my son had a file in the Holy of Holies, the central computer room in the company offices at B.G. Airport. For twenty minutes he kept me waiting on the line until he informed me that he was unable to access the details because his code wasn't confidential enough. I asked him if by any chance his seventeen-year-old daughter had become unintentionally pregnant, and he admitted that this was the case. I told him that I would perform a pirate abortion on her, on the condition that he supplied me with potentially relevant information. We arranged to meet at the dead of night in the underground parking lot of the building where I used to live. His daughter was already in the car, her legs open, and there was nothing I could do but confirm her death. Since she was dead, her father refused to give me the confidential information, but my blood was boiling and I screamed into the dark, dank parking lot:

"I've had it already with all this philanthropic mystery! Who's behind it?"

The man did not reply, he was looking at his daughter's purple face. I shook him the way you shake somebody when you just can't take it any more—he was really getting on my nerves.

"Out with it, or I'll smash your face in," I said.

"Give me five minutes," he said eventually and went to hide behind one of the parking lot's numbered pillars, as if I couldn't see him, where he said something into a two-way radio. A few minutes later he came up to me and said dryly:

"The man, the connecting link, the person in charge of Pan-T business in Dolly City, is at this moment playing squash in the Dolly City Squash and Billiard Club."

I put my hands in my pockets and broke into a quick run in the direction of the club, which was located in the city's aesthetic quarter.

At the entrance to the club they asked me if I was a Kurd.

"Why?" I asked.

"No Kurds allowed."

One of the experiences provided by life on this planet is the "floor-rag effect." Sometimes you see something in the distance, from a certain crooked angle, and it looks like an eagle, like a stuffed God-knows-what, like a sketch of the devil's insides—but when you come closer you see that it's only a floor-rag or a shred of rubber tire or a squashed, rotten lump of cardboard. In Dolly City it often happens that you think something is something, and in the end it turns out that it isn't.

To someone like me, who can be driven crazy by the fact that parallel lines meet in infinity, because it's beyond her comprehension, someone who thinks it makes sense to call the fire brigade nonstop because of the mere *possibility* that the house might burn down, someone who hears the alert and the all-safe signals sounding simultaneously—encountering the floor-rag effect is routine, and she experiences it dozens of times a day.

Over the course of the years, I gained experience. I learned that in most cases there was no real point in trying to unravel the true nature of the mystery. With the passing of yet more years, I developed a firmer grip on reality, and often I no longer bother to come closer in order to get to the bottom of things. In other words, I don't advance towards the eagle, but simply say to myself: There you are, eagle or old floor rag—and continue on my way.

When I went into the squash club, I knew in advance that you couldn't even call it unraveling a mystery, but at the most checking something out, on the scale of checking out the state of your bank balance. I wasn't mistaken, and as I got closer it became clear: indeed, a floor-rag.

The Third Man was a lawyer, an old and conceited friend of my parents, Egyptian in origin like them, and an ex-member of the same kibbutz that they were members of for a few months, when they first came to this country in the early fifties.

At that moment I felt so chagrined that I was no longer even interested in tying up the loose ends. What good will it do you? I asked myself. Sometimes just knowing some fact or other, even if that fact leads somewhere, is fifty times more depressing than not knowing it. It's like the feeling you get when you're forced to listen to something. In Dolly City people have understood this, and so they keep their big mouths shut, they spare each other their troubles—and rightly so!

Even though lawyers and doctors are more or less the same species—both of us belong to those concerned with the maintenance of the human race—I don't like lawyers, or as my late mother used to say, I'm not in sympathy with them. To tell the truth, I loathe lawyers. All that act of theirs, with their black gowns as if they're some kind of handsome vampires, knights of justice—as far as I'm concerned, you can shove it up your ass.

In Dolly City the lawyers aren't made of rubber, or of chewing gum either—they're just lawyers, and like lawyers everywhere they keep on saying, And inasmuch as . . . and inasmuch as . . . and it makes me sick. The way they build up a whole case on that and inasmuch as of theirs—it's utterly nauseating. Those black cloaks of theirs and those casserole-dish hats on their heads are fifty times more ridiculous than any doctor's white coat. As far as I'm concerned, a lawyer screwing a doctor is a horror movie. Him in his black gown, and her in her virginal white coat, they fuck, and it's a chessboard. Ha, ha. Apart from which, with all those gowns and coats, how do they manage to penetrate each other at all? Ha.

The day before my father died, this lawyer came into his room in oncology at Ichilov, held his vein-riddled hand, and said to him:

"It'll be all right, you'll get better."

"God is great," replied my father, who'd never so much as glanced at the sky in his life, except when Pan-T planes were flying overhead. His loyalty to the national airline was sky-high—it broke all records. When a TWA plane flew overhead, or even an Arkia plane, he would sense, with a sixth sense, that it wasn't one of ours, and wouldn't throw it a glance. The calendars we had at home were always the huge colored ones printed by Pan-T. On the rear window of our green Fiat 127 my father stuck a sticker: Support Pan-T flights on the Shabbat. On the cupboard, where the china dolls acquired on family trips all over the world once stood, was a two-sided sign, with Pan-T in English on one side and Hebrew on the other.

My father was active in the union during the workers' strikes. This man, who never opened his mouth at home except to say hello when he came in from work at a quarter to five, fought with the fervor of a militant revolutionary for the rights of the workers, who in the depths of their hearts despised him.

If he got a phone call at home, it was sure to be from Pan-T. My sister and I would watch him giving those people everything he had. It wasn't a ritual, that whole Pan-T thing, far from it, it was in our blood, a matter of life and death. It's no coincidence that we, my sister and I, both chose professions that demand self-sacrifice and total commitment. With my father it was out of idealism, with her it was out of altruism, and with me—out of madness.

The lawyer sat in a white towel-robe and asked me if I needed anything. I didn't answer him, but my mind was working overtime. I guessed that during that last visit to my father the dying man had asked him to take charge of the education of my children, if and when I had any. Apparently he just didn't trust me.

Like all my parents' friends and relatives, the lawyer too had felt nothing but contempt for my way of life and my studies. He belonged to the large group of Egyptian Jews who refused to believe that I was a doctor, and who were convinced that for all eight years of my studies in Katmandu I'd been busy screwing everyone in town, or at least going down on them.

He lit a cigar as fat as his face and said that he was now at liberty to reveal to me: my father had not left all his money to the Society for the War against Cancer, but also to the naval training of my son, when and if he were born, and if it were a girl—to her training as a professional dancer. The lawyer said that at the time when he died, the airline company agreed—on condition that the family wouldn't take my father's compensation money at once—to invest the money on the stock market, take the profits for itself, and dole out the sums necessary to cover the expenses of the child's education from time to time, as well as a token donation once a year on the annual fund-raising day of the Cancer Society. In other words, my father preferred to let Pan-T juggle his money, as long as it didn't land in my lap. The dead man didn't know that I'd become a doctor, and he'd kept me from getting my hands on the money.

I returned to the street, multiplying and dividing, extracting roots from all kinds of numbers, and getting more and more confused. My feet carried me to the Pan-T offices in Dolly City again. I went up to the accounting department and sat down with the clerk to calculate. We took the sum total of the compensation money that was composed of my father's last salary times 150 percent, times thirty-two years that he worked for Pan-T, and added the small sum which I wrote on my mother's blank check—the good woman hated open checks and I hurried to close it for her. The sum total, minus open brackets (a donation of fifty shekels a year to the Cancer Society, times fifty-six, my father's age, plus the cost of Son's education at the Academy for Brutal Seamanship, plus the cost of a simple fishing boat, for the purpose of ensuring his income, plus all the family's free flights during the years of my father's employment at Pan-T, close brackets), the sum total was . . .

The resulting sum was supposed to be invested in the stock market, with Pan-T acting as the broker—but in the end it came out minus a very large sum—in other words, I still owed them.

"Minus seventeen million five hundred and forty-six shekels," said the clerk in the end.

"Are you sure?" I mumbled.

"There's nothing in this world more decisive than numbers. A pistol with a nine-millimeter bullet is a pistol with a nine-millimeter bullet. There's no two ways about it."

Among my possessions was an old checkbook from the days when I had an account at the Bavly Housing Estate branch of the Discount Bank.

"Can you divide it into . . . three payments?"

She made a face, as if her father owned the company.

"What can I say," she said, and I scribbled the sums on the checks and gave them to her.

When I walked away from the beige building I felt calm. Although the checks had nothing to back them up, it was all completely theoretical, I felt that at long last I'd been relieved of a heavy burden. I strolled over to the Yarkon River to go for a sail, and behind one of the eucalyptus trees I suddenly thought I saw my mother crying, but it was only an old scarecrow. When all was said and done, the woman had donated her body to science, not to me, I thought, trying to picture her face in my mind. In her last days her face was as furrowed as a field ravaged by some demented plough. All my madness was reflected in the old woman's face.

For the first time since her death I felt something approaching sorrow. At the same time, I couldn't stand the thought of some medical student digging into her appendix, but she asked for it—so she better enjoy it!

Time passed like it always does. First the years, then the months, the days, the hours, the minutes, and last but not least—the seconds. I was already resigned to living with this cancer I had in my soul, yes, you could certainly say that I was suffering from cancer of the soul, with possibilities multiplying inside me instead of cells, and parts of the whole turning into essences in and of themselves. True—and this must be said, there are things that are better said than left unsaid, you have to spew them out and not keep them bottled up—my mental state had improved since the period of my hospitalization. When I walked down the street, the path, or wherever, I no longer felt that I was insane, and I'd also learned to live with my fractured memory.

My only son was already fifteen, or so he claimed in his frequent letters. He also sent me Polaroid snapshots of himself waving the Israeli flag on the open sea, or standing to attention at morning roll call on the floating school. I shoved all the snapshots inside my locker at the railway station. Maybe one day, I said to myself, I'll make him an album, who knows.

I could have been proud of him, his letters showed more than a spark of sanity. The boy was happy—he was chosen as outstanding cadet. I didn't know what I was supposed to feel. I knew that life was tricky, it would outsmart you in a jiffy, you had to watch out for it—it could happen that after the kid was made outstanding cadet, he'd suddenly die of cancer, just like that, for the sake of nature's equilibrium. I knew that nature had to go on, and that it didn't let anyone off, we were all its obedient drones, and that if we didn't resist it the most we could expect was to come up for air once in a while—and whenever I detected a note of happiness in my son's letters my heart filled with anxiety.

Every now and then I wrote him letters in which I encouraged him and concluded by telling him to keep a stiff upper lip and giving him a lot of advice about how to avoid illnesses and what to eat at sea in order not to throw up. But my main advice concerned how to cope at school and how to keep from letting the pressure get him down and upset his peace of mind.

I knew that the Academy of Brutal Seamanship wasn't Tel Aviv University, or the University of Katmandu either. I knew, although he never said a word about it, that he had to hide his many scars from the eyes of his officers and fellow cadets. I said to myself—the scars are one thing, he can say that he once tried hara-kiri, but what about the map of the Land of Israel on his back? It's obvious that somebody else put it there. Apart from which—he'd returned to the '67 borders, and that's nothing to brag about in a military academy these days.

Interestingly enough, by the way, I'd never, never heard or read even the faintest, tiniest hint of complaint from the boy about the fact that I'd cut him up so often, and all for nothing—after all I could have killed him, and had exposed him to terrible dangers.

In the insane asylum I'd asked what I should do, what I should say if and when the child asked what I'd performed on him. They told me that I should explain that I had a problem with aggression, that my aggressions took control of me, instead of my common sense. They told me to ask his forgiveness and to "let time do the rest."

The kid was okay. He accepted it all naturally, as if it was all part of some distant childhood. He was open and uninhibited. He sent me a bunch of rude and rollicking sea shanties and claimed that he'd composed them himself—but I doubt it.

One day, maybe it was April, maybe May, I'm fed up with remembering dates all the time, I freaked out because I couldn't remember the boy's face. That's it, I've lost him, I thought and sunk into an unbearable depression. I was here, and he—there. And what could I do about it? Nothing. What kind of a thing is motherhood if you can't take care of your child nonstop, one hundred percent? Motherhood is when a mother bends down and whispers into her child's ear: "Be careful when you cross the street! Be careful, the streetcar drivers are maniacs. Don't go swimming in the pool in winter, watch out for child molesters. Don't eat junk food—it gives you cancer."

I went to the Hilton Beach to blow a kiss, maybe it would reach my son, but deep down I know my kiss wouldn't get far. Otherwise there would have been dozens of other mothers standing on the shore and sending kisses to their loved ones. To myself, I began to admit that my whole conception was wrong. I'd worked like a dog, in vain. I'd built dams in places where there wasn't even a river, and persuaded myself that flashes of light were rushing waters I've successfully trapped.

The globe revolved, and I was dizzy with hunger because I was barely eking out a living. People discovered bran, prunes, glycerin suppositories, and I, as an enemaist, had no more work. What a miserable time it was. I spent a lot of time sitting in parks and looking at the bushes, at the couples in the bushes, at the birds, at two bulls fucking.

Winds blew, the trees behaved like a gang of clowns having their hair pulled. On the news they said that a lot of people were now going to Nagasaki, that Nagasaki was now the safest place in the world, because according to sacred Probability, the youth's golden idol, an atom bomb isn't dropped on the same place more than once every hundred years.

One twilight hour I was sitting in the park, the sun was in the west, red and sinking like an ancient culture. Darkness gradually descended on Dolly City, and swallowed all its colors.

Suddenly a light flashed in the black sky and I thought, here goes, Dolly, gallons of water will come pouring down on your head again. But I was wrong. Additional flashes of light revealed a cloudy sky covered with hundreds, maybe thousands of gray and black French Air Force planes. The descendents of the Gauls, the comrades and successors of Saint-Exupery, had arrived with their most up-to-date weapons to wipe out the inhabitants of Dolly City, and thousands of animals were parachuted down, dogs and jackals and foxes infected mainly with rabies, but also with typhus and other serious diseases. The animals spread through the city like swarms of locusts, and people began to vomit and fall twitching to the ground, and all kinds of youth movements began setting up field hospitals, and heralds walked around requesting doctors from all ethnic communities to present themselves for job interviews. I said to myself, Dolly, this is your big day, everyone's sick, everyone's dying. I ran to the job interview. I got the job.

Again I found myself in a laboratory with quite decent equipment, mixing wine with blood, battle rations with blood units. The town was full of rumors that the French were only the tip of the iceberg, that they were only German vassals, and that it was the Germans who were actually behind all these air attacks—since if a German told a Frenchman to jump off the roof, he'd jump off the roof. They said that the French mercenaries wanted to wipe out the entire population of Israel, filling the whole of the coastal plain with gleaming white lavatories of the finest export quality.

People talked about the Germans and cursed them all the time, it really turned them on. In the closed wards of the many insane asylums in Dolly City there was a big demand for German POW's, to show them who's their daddy. It got out that a certain POW, Friedrich, had fallen into the hands of a few manic-depressives who sodomized him, vomited on him, and then went through his pockets where they found American chewing gum, and ate it all up.

I hardly got any sleep. I worked round the clock. I even agreed to go to the post office and buy stamps, so that the wounded soldiers arriving in droves from the battlefield could send letters home to their mothers.

The air raids grew heavier, and the French began dropping shit-bombs on us, there was so much shit flying around that it was hard to understand where they were getting it all from.

I heard someone say they simply liked eating, they were a nation that just loved to eat, and it was all down to their superior metabolisms.

Every few days people arrived, soldiers and civilians, who'd been hit by an atom bomb. Then everyone stopped working, a hush fell on the hospital. The performance of the atom bombs was truly amazing. Sometimes people came in without heads, but with eyes. Some of them came in without legs, but walking, with shoes full of mud. And the funniest of all were the ones without waists, whose upper and lower halves were connected by association.

My contact with my son was completely cut off. It was months since I'd received a letter from him. I repressed it. I commanded myself: Forget, Dolly, forget. But one day I said, enough, I asked for a pass from the head of the department, and I went to see the city's military magistrate. I asked a crop-haired secretary for information on the location and well-being of the destroyer on which my son's school was situated. She didn't know.

"So what do you suggest I do?" I asked. "Really, I'm asking you. Tell me."

"I don't know what to say. Look at the map of the world, and try to find your son according to your maternal instincts."

"Thank you," I said, disappointed, and headed for the door.

"Listen," she called after me, "maybe you should wait for the military magistrate after all, maybe he'll finish quickly. He's with the mayor, you know."

"Okay," I said.

I waited for a quarter of an hour until the door opened, and the mayor of Dolly City, who's also the owner of a detergent factory, came out, buttoning up his fly. I went into the dark room. On the floor lay the magistrate, naked and limp, staring at the concave plastic ceiling. I asked him to help me.

I sat for five hours in the magistrate's room, while he put on his underpants, lit a cigarette, and sat in front of the computer trying to find some information according to the boy's identity number. I sat next to him and waited quietly, drinking cup after cup of coffee with sugar and sweetener, until my head was bursting from the pressure.

The magistrate did everything humanly possible, I know that. He sweated, he asked me to give him a shot of Benzedrine in the ass, he couldn't keep his eyes open. The guy was exhausted, he fell asleep on his desk and I covered him up. I waited.

The sun sank. I must have run to the toilet twenty-five times to rid myself of all the coffee I drank.

The military magistrate's offices in Dolly City are located in a very high building erected on the ruins of the Shalom Tower department store. The whole of Dolly City in all its ugliness was spread out below me. I glanced up—there were no planes in the sky, and I remembered that today was the 14th of July, and the French were all going down on each other and dancing in the streets to commemorate the Bastilles. Those characters think that if they gave humanity all that crap about the separation of powers, the innate goodness of man—all that saccharine bullshit—then they've left their mark and done their part. But as far as I'm concerned they didn't do a thing except invent Napoleon who thought he was Napoleon, and all that ridiculous pretense of the Gardens of Versailles and the powder on Marie Antoinette's nose.

I returned from the summery balcony to the magistrate's room. He'd woken up and gone back to work at full steam, his piercing eyes fixed on the computer screen.

"Anything new?" I asked him, coming in with another cup of steaming coffee in my hands. His face was clouded. He looked as if he'd just taken a punch to the jaw that hadn't yet turned his face blue.

"The destroyer was sunk," he said, "I'm terribly sorry."

"Sunk?" My hand was shaking, the coffee spilled on the carpet.

"Who did it?" I asked, as if it mattered.

"The Belgians."

"The Belgians? I thought they stayed out of this."

"They did it by mistake, they thought it was a French ship. A tragic mistake. I don't know how to console you, I really don't know."

I took the cup of coffee and smashed it on the screen. I sank to the depths of hell in my grief.

The magistrate asked me to spend the night with him, but I preferred committing suicide.

I stood on the bridge about to put an end to it all. I thought about all the operations and vaccinations I'd given him, and how he'd gone and died on me so senselessly. The Belgians! Of all people!

I opened my mouth like in *The Scream* by Munch. I set one foot on the balustrade of the bridge, then the other, I was about to jump, but at that instant I saw a man dressed in rags running towards me and shouting:

"No! Don't do it!"

Isn't God sick of that gimmick yet? I wondered, and jumped.

The water was a catastrophe. The crocodiles slapped me with their wagging tails. I said to myself—this is the last straw, soon this chapter will come to an end, and after that an eternal interlude, and indeed, something under the water's surface was pulling me down to the depths, and I was sure that I was already dead, but when we touched bottom I saw that it was a diver dressed in a black diving-suit. The diver pulled off his mask, and before my eyes floated my son, my own Son, flesh of my flesh, from head to toe.

A crowd of onlookers gathered on the bank. My son got out of his suit, and both of us sat on the grass to get a bit of sun. My teeth chattered. What an amazing coincidence, I thought, that precisely the most improbable thing from a statistical point of view—happened.

On the bank I asked my son:

"So, the story about the destroyer going down wasn't true?"

"I don't know."

"What do you mean?"

"I was lucky—I volunteered. I went out on a raft to look for mine-bearing fish."

"Aha, so the destroyer was sunk and you were saved?"

"Something like that."

His face was burnt by the sun, scarred and ripped apart. He looked a mess. I wanted to fix him up, to give him a total makeover, but I no longer felt capable of cutting him up. He was no longer a child, and he probably wouldn't have agreed anyway. I concentrated on a deep gash on his left cheek. On no account could I remember when I'd cut him there, or why.

"What are your plans?" I asked him.

"What are my plans?"

"Yes."

He looked at a woman jumping into the river, and said:

"I think I'll go and rescue her. I belong to the river police, a new secret police that saves suicides from drowning."

"Really?" I didn't know how to take this at all.

He jumped into the water and swam towards the woman. The crocodile tails lashed at him too, but he tied them together in a granny knot, just as I'd tied the rabbits' ears together during my days of glory. For a long time he struggled with the woman, who tried to drown them both and to throw herself into the crocodiles' jaws. He succeeded in overcoming her, but *très bizarre*—a few meters before reaching the bank he let the woman go, and she drowned. He came out of the water and smiled at me.

"What happened? Did you get fed up halfway through?"

"Yes," he replied. "She was too desperate. Maybe it's because of the weather. The weather's been lousy lately."

My son hospitalized me in a shelter for the elderly in Dolly City, even though I was only forty-five and in full control of myself and never wet my bed. He told me that he was hospitalizing me out of a sense of poetic justice. He himself tried for a time to get a job in the F.B.I. but it didn't work out. We were almost out of touch. He'd freed himself of me, no doubt about that, he was his own master, and I no longer troubled myself about him. I concluded that whatever would be would be, what more could I do.

One fine day, to tell the truth it was on my forty-ninth birthday, I saw one of the old women holding a newspaper with a picture of my son on the front page, looking serious as hell.

"Let me have a look at the paper for a minute," I asked her, but she refused.

"Ma'am," I said, "I'll give it back to you straight away."

"I don't believe in mankind," she shouted, "I don't believe you."

"Then you hold it, okay?"

She turned the front page towards me and I read: "Attempt by young crank to hijack Pan-T plane to Luxembourg foiled." I glanced quickly through the item in the newspaper, which the old woman was holding in her trembling hand. The investigators couldn't understand how the young man had succeeded in overcoming the strictest security measures in the world. I went on reading, eager to find out what had happened to him. I understood that he'd been caught, that he'd escaped, that they'd shot him, that he'd been wounded in the back (they never said where in the back—the

Jezreel Valley? Or maybe it was bang on Dolly City), that he'd gone on running, that helicopters were searching for him in all the craters and valleys of the Gobi Desert, but the chances of finding him, they said, were extremely slim. It didn't bother me one little bit that the kid hadn't succeeded in hijacking the plane. That was all nonsense. My heart pounded in my breast with excitement, I could really feel it expand and contract, and my brain danced inside the receptacle of my skull. I was worried about the boy, but I wasn't hysterical. I knew that after everything I'd done to him— a bullet or a knife in the back were nothing he couldn't handle.

AFTERWORD

Dolly City is an astonishing novel. It leaves some readers en-
thralled, some stunned, and others intimidated. Orly Castel-
Bloom told me that, in the months following the Israeli publication of the novel in 1992, people who recognized her as its author
were actually afraid of her. Castel-Bloom's writing—confronta-
tional, fearless, and disconcertingly funny—often evokes such
visceral reactions. Now, nearly two decades after its appearance
first shocked the Israeli reading public, the novel remains as pro-
vocative and powerful as it was then.

Born in Tel Aviv in 1960 to French-speaking Egyptian Jewish parents, Orly Castel-Bloom spoke only French during the
first years of her life. She studied film at Tel Aviv University for
one year and theater for another at the Beit Zvi theater school.
She started publishing in 1987. By the time *Dolly City* appeared,
Israeli critics had already been debating the merits of Castel-
Bloom's writing for five years. Her first collection of short stories,
Lo Rahok mi-Merkaz ha-Ir (Not Far from the Center of Town,
1987) evoked much critical controversy, particularly regarding

its unconventional language and style. Her second collection, *Sviva Oyenet* (Hostile Surroundings, 1989), and her first novel, *Heykhan Ani Nimtset* (Where Am I, 1990), confirmed the originality of her voice, but some critics still questioned the "literary" value of Castel-Bloom's writing: the unadorned, conversational Hebrew of her stories, peppered with English expressions, was labeled flat and therefore inadequate for literary expression. Her unsentimental and sometimes absurd characters were considered devoid of humanity and incapable of evoking the reader's sympathy or interest.

The publication of *Dolly City*, while it did not dispel entirely the questions regarding Castel-Bloom's literary merit, established her as a prominent figure, impossible and irresponsible to ignore. Gershon Shaked, an influential literary critic, deemed that Castel-Bloom had "done nothing less than change the face of Hebrew fiction." The esteemed author S. Yizhar praised her writing, and the prominent critic Dan Miron declared her to be one of the most interesting writers of her generation. *Dolly City* was reviewed in all the major Israeli newspapers. Adi Ophir, in his review for *Ma'ariv*, recommended that readers read the novel three or four times: first, "to absorb the shock"; second, to understand how and why Dolly does what she does; third, to connect Dolly's world to one's own; and fourth, to get to the bottom of Castel-Bloom's idiosyncratic use of language. In a review in *Ha'aretz*, Ariel Hirschfeld declared that *Dolly City* constitutes a new Israeli-Hebrew dictionary, challenging all accepted definitions and values. Indeed, *Dolly City* helped establish Castel-Bloom as one of the most important living writers of Hebrew, compared to a diverse array of authors from Dostoyevsky to Kafka. Though not everyone agrees on the merits of Castel-Bloom's writing, it leaves no one indifferent.

By now, four novels and four short story collections later, the centrality of *Dolly City* in the world of Israeli letters is undisputed. This is somewhat incongruous, given that the novel is itself an attack on all forms of authority, political, social, or linguistic. Zionist ideology, represented here by Dolly's acquaintance Gordon (a parody of the Russian Zionist A. D. Gordon), is tolerated but not taken seriously. The Holocaust, the memory and memorializing of which is a primary component of collective identity in Israel, is presented in *Dolly City* as a crime warranting bloody vengeance, and also as a means of exclusion of non-European Jews like Dolly from the nation's consciousness. The novel's critical confrontation with Israeli society leads it to raise questions about gender as well. Dolly's obsessive and fiercely independent motherhood is complicated by the fact that her son's paternity is unknown and by the mystery of her own father's death. In Israeli literature, which historically has been preoccupied with fathers and sons, the dearth of literal and metaphoric fathers in this novel makes a significant statement. The language, too, contributes to the novel's iconoclasm. Some readers dislike what has been called Castel-Bloom's "thin Hebrew," which they see as stripped of the richness and depth of the "literary" Hebrew considered the epitome of Zionist ideals. A close reading of her stories and novels, however, shows that there is more to Castel-Bloom's use of language than meets the eye: it is informed by biblical allusions, clever word games, and an awareness of the ideological dynamics of language. Moreover, her Hebrew resonates with readers because it acknowledges and incorporates its own perpetual development through television, slang, new technologies, and the languages of immigrants. Not surprisingly, Castel-Bloom's "thin Hebrew" has spawned more than a few admiring imitations.

One need not know Hebrew to get a sense of how revolutionary *Dolly City* is. The prose pummels the reader. Dolly, by turns apathetic and enraged, is articulate and perhaps overly perceptive. "Madness is a predator," she observes. "Its food is the soul. It takes over the soul as rapidly as our forces occupied Judea, Samaria, and the Gaza Strip in 1967. [. . .] And if a state like the State of Israel can't control the Arabs in the territories, how can anybody expect me, a private individual, to control the occupied territories inside myself?" (95–96). She explicitly relates the chaos within her to the political mayhem that plagues her environment. Violence reigns in her city. And a strange city it is: dystopic, fantastic, phantasmagoric, nightmarish—Dolly City is unlike any other setting in Hebrew literature. At once Tel Aviv and every other city in the world, Dolly City recalls the alienating metropolis that is by now a familiar setting of modernist writing, at the same time adding terrifying new features to this landscape. It is a city whose inhabitants are not only lonely, anxious, and unfriendly, but also deeply depressed and murderously violent. Dolly's own aggressive tendencies, which drive her to surreptitiously inject unwitting passersby with morphine, murder a host of German orphans, castrate her psychiatrist, and more, reflect the violence of her city and affect every aspect of her relationships with others, from strangers on the street to her own son. No recognizable ethical or moral code governs Dolly City, and nothing is too sacred to escape the blade of Castel-Bloom's pen. This is a world where everything has lost its significance—Dachau in Dolly City is just a word on an old plank—so the reader must question everything.

The violence that is so prevalent in *Dolly City* is related to two particular overlapping concerns that Castel-Bloom addresses, motherhood and the nation. The experience of motherhood as expressed in *Dolly City* is at once universally human and specifically Israeli, as attested by two of the most striking images in the novel: Dolly's son glued to her back and the map of the Land of Israel she carves on his back. The first image speaks to phenomena that cross linguistic, geographic, and cultural boundaries: it magnifies the fears and concerns that are part of every mother's experience, and casts the son as a burden the mother must bear. The latter image, an explicitly political, fleshly cartography, addresses the idiosyncrasies of Israeli motherhood, subject to the demands of national identity and, more concretely, of the military, in which every secular Israeli Jew—male and female—is required to serve at age eighteen. Dolly's *raison d'être* is to protect her son: "I wanted to be in command on all fronts, and what's wrong with that?" she demands. "I'm not entitled to demand sovereignty over the defense of my son?" (52). The vocabulary of war is not coincidental in this context. Dolly's son's eventual conscription to the Academy of Brutal Seamanship denies her "sovereignty" over his "defense," even as it liberates him from his obsessively protective mother. The mother/son interaction is one of many in the novel marked by aggression, paranoia, and impatience. Perhaps *Dolly City*'s most chilling accomplishment is laying bare a society in which not only politics and war but also interpersonal relations are exceedingly violent. A mother cuts into her son's flesh; suicides regularly plummet earthward from skyscrapers; vehicles collide into each other relentlessly; Jews crucify non-Jews in the street. Subject to Dolly's keen gaze, these violent social relations erupt on the surface of Dolly City itself in the form of cancerous tumors. Dolly's response—a frenzied attempt to cure the city, followed by indifference—parallels the broader postmodern concern at the heart of the novel: contemporary society is sick and there is no cure in sight.

It would be a mistake, however, to allow this bleak assessment to overshadow other qualities of the novel. Perhaps one of the most effective resources in Castel-Bloom's critical arsenal is her sometimes macabre sense of humor. Despite the seriousness of the issues it confronts, *Dolly City* is a very funny book. Like the novel and two collections of short stories by Castel-Bloom that preceded it, *Dolly City* uses black humor, satire, parody, and sarcasm to express anxiety and to criticize social norms. Castel-Bloom, like her contemporary Etgar Keret, finds new discursive possibilities in humor: the language of humor allows her to make the banal original, and the horrible somewhat palatable.

Dalkey Archive's new edition of *Dolly City* at last makes this important novel available to English-language readers worldwide, filling a lacuna in the library of Israeli works available in translation. As we move into the second decade of the millennium, the relevance and acuity of *Dolly City* become increasingly apparent, not only for Israel, but for contemporary society as a whole.

Hirschfeld, Ariel. "Tehomot me-ahorey Ets ha-Shesek" [The Abyss Behind the Loquat Tree], *Ha'aretz* (May 25, 1992).

Miron, Dan. "Mashehu al Orly Castel-Bloom" [A Word on Orly Castel-Bloom], *Al Ha-mishmar* (June 16, 1989).

Ophir, Adi. "Dolly City," *Ma'ariv* (April 10, 1992).

Shaked, Gershon. *Modern Hebrew Fiction* (Bloomington and Indianapolis: Indiana University Press, 2000).

KAREN GRUMBERG, 2010

HEBREW LITERATURE SERIES

The Hebrew Literature Series at Dalkey Archive Press makes available major works of Hebrew-language literature in English translation. Featuring exceptional authors at the forefront of Hebrew letters, the series aims to introduce the rich intellectual and aesthetic diversity of contemporary Hebrew writing and culture to English-language readers.

This series is published in collaboration with the Institute for the Translation of Hebrew Literature, at www.ithl.org.il. Thanks are also due to the Office of Cultural Affairs at the Consulate General of Israel, NY, for their support.

ORLY CASTEL-BLOOM was born in Tel Aviv in 1960 and is a leading voice in contemporary Hebrew literature. She is the author of thirteen books and was twice the recipient of the Prime Minister's Prize. *Dolly City* has been included in UNESCO's Collection of Representative Works.

DALYA BILU lives in Jerusalem and has been awarded a number of prizes for her translation work, including the Israeli Ministry of Culture Prize for Translation, and the Jewish Book Council Award for Hebrew-English Translation.

PETROS ABATZOGLOU, *What Does Mrs. Freeman Want?*
MICHAL AJVAZ, *The Golden Age.*
The Other City.
PIERRE ALBERT-BIROT, *Grabinoulor.*
YUZ ALESHKOVSKY, *Kangaroo.*
FELIPE ALFAU, *Chromos.*
Locos.
IVAN ÂNGELO, *The Celebration.*
The Tower of Glass.
DAVID ANTIN, *Talking.*
ANTÓNIO LOBO ANTUNES, *Knowledge of Hell.*
ALAIN ARIAS-MISSON, *Theatre of Incest.*
IFTIKHAR ARIF AND WAQAS KHWAJA, EDS., *Modern Poetry of Pakistan.*
JOHN ASHBERY AND JAMES SCHUYLER, *A Nest of Ninnies.*
HEIMRAD BÄCKER, *transcript.*
DJUNA BARNES, *Ladies Almanack.*
Ryder.
JOHN BARTH, *LETTERS.*
Sabbatical.
DONALD BARTHELME, *The King.*
Paradise.
SVETISLAV BASARA, *Chinese Letter.*
RENÉ BELLETTO, *Dying.*
MARK BINELLI, *Sacco and Vanzetti Must Die!*
ANDREI BITOV, *Pushkin House.*
ANDREJ BLATNIK, *You Do Understand.*
LOUIS PAUL BOON, *Chapel Road.*
My Little War.
Summer in Termuren.
ROGER BOYLAN, *Killoyle.*
IGNÁCIO DE LOYOLA BRANDÃO, *Anonymous Celebrity.*
The Good-Bye Angel.
Teeth under the Sun.
Zero.
BONNIE BREMSER, *Troia: Mexican Memoirs.*
CHRISTINE BROOKE-ROSE, *Amalgamemnon.*
BRIGID BROPHY, *In Transit.*
MEREDITH BROSNAN, *Mr. Dynamite.*
GERALD L. BRUNS, *Modern Poetry and the Idea of Language.*
EVGENY BUNIMOVICH AND J. KATES, EDS., *Contemporary Russian Poetry: An Anthology.*
GABRIELLE BURTON, *Heartbreak Hotel.*
MICHEL BUTOR, *Degrees.*
Mobile.
Portrait of the Artist as a Young Ape.
G. CABRERA INFANTE, *Infante's Inferno.*
Three Trapped Tigers.
JULIETA CAMPOS, *The Fear of Losing Eurydice.*
ANNE CARSON, *Eros the Bittersweet.*
ORLY CASTEL-BLOOM, *Dolly City.*
CAMILO JOSÉ CELA, *Christ versus Arizona.*
The Family of Pascual Duarte.
The Hive.
LOUIS-FERDINAND CÉLINE, *Castle to Castle.*
Conversations with Professor Y.
London Bridge.

Normance.
North.
Rigadoon.
HUGO CHARTERIS, *The Tide Is Right.*
JEROME CHARYN, *The Tar Baby.*
MARC CHOLODENKO, *Mordechai Schamz.*
JOSHUA COHEN, *Witz.*
EMILY HOLMES COLEMAN, *The Shutter of Snow.*
ROBERT COOVER, *A Night at the Movies.*
STANLEY CRAWFORD, *Log of the S.S. The Mrs Unguentine.*
Some Instructions to My Wife.
ROBERT CREELEY, *Collected Prose.*
RENÉ CREVEL, *Putting My Foot in It.*
RALPH CUSACK, *Cadenza.*
SUSAN DAITCH, *L.C.*
Storytown.
NICHOLAS DELBANCO, *The Count of Concord.*
NIGEL DENNIS, *Cards of Identity.*
PETER DIMOCK, *A Short Rhetoric for Leaving the Family.*
ARIEL DORFMAN, *Konfidenz.*
COLEMAN DOWELL, *The Houses of Children.*
Island People.
Too Much Flesh and Jabez.
ARKADII DRAGOMOSHCHENKO, *Dust.*
RIKKI DUCORNET, *The Complete Butcher's Tales.*
The Fountains of Neptune.
The Jade Cabinet.
The One Marvelous Thing.
Phosphor in Dreamland.
The Stain.
The Word "Desire."
WILLIAM EASTLAKE, *The Bamboo Bed.*
Castle Keep.
Lyric of the Circle Heart.
JEAN ECHENOZ, *Chopin's Move.*
STANLEY ELKIN, *A Bad Man.*
Boswell: A Modern Comedy.
Criers and Kibitzers, Kibitzers and Criers.
The Dick Gibson Show.
The Franchiser.
George Mills.
The Living End.
The MacGuffin.
The Magic Kingdom.
Mrs. Ted Bliss.
The Rabbi of Lud.
Van Gogh's Room at Arles.
ANNIE ERNAUX, *Cleaned Out.*
LAUREN FAIRBANKS, *Muzzle Thyself.*
Sister Carrie.
LESLIE A. FIEDLER, *Love and Death in the American Novel.*
JUAN FILLOY, *Op Oloop.*
GUSTAVE FLAUBERT, *Bouvard and Pécuchet.*
KASS FLEISHER, *Talking out of School.*
FORD MADOX FORD, *The March of Literature.*
JON FOSSE, *Aliss at the Fire.*
Melancholy.

FOR A FULL LIST OF PUBLICATIONS, VISIT:
www.dalkeyarchive.com

SELECTED DALKEY ARCHIVE PAPERBACKS

MAX FRISCH, *I'm Not Stiller.*
Man in the Holocene.
CARLOS FUENTES, *Christopher Unborn.*
Distant Relations.
Terra Nostra.
Where the Air Is Clear.
JANICE GALLOWAY, *Foreign Parts.*
The Trick Is to Keep Breathing.
WILLIAM H. GASS, *Cartesian Sonata and Other Novellas.*
Finding a Form.
A Temple of Texts.
The Tunnel.
Willie Masters' Lonesome Wife.
GÉRARD GAVARRY, *Hoppla! 1 2 3.*
ETIENNE GILSON,
The Arts of the Beautiful.
Forms and Substances in the Arts.
C. S. GISCOMBE, *Giscome Road.*
Here.
Prairie Style.
DOUGLAS GLOVER, *Bad News of the Heart.*
The Enamoured Knight.
WITOLD GOMBROWICZ,
A Kind of Testament.
KAREN ELIZABETH GORDON,
The Red Shoes.
GEORGI GOSPODINOV, *Natural Novel.*
JUAN GOYTISOLO, *Count Julian.*
Juan the Landless.
Makbara.
Marks of Identity.
PATRICK GRAINVILLE, *The Cave of Heaven.*
HENRY GREEN, *Back.*
Blindness.
Concluding.
Doting.
Nothing.
JIŘÍ GRUŠA, *The Questionnaire.*
GABRIEL GUDDING,
Rhode Island Notebook.
MELA HARTWIG, *Am I a Redundant Human Being?*
JOHN HAWKES, *The Passion Artist.*
Whistlejacket.
ALEKSANDAR HEMON, ED.,
Best European Fiction.
AIDAN HIGGINS, *A Bestiary.*
Balcony of Europe.
Bornholm Night-Ferry.
Darkling Plain: Texts for the Air.
Flotsam and Jetsam.
Langrishe, Go Down.
Scenes from a Receding Past.
Windy Arbours.
KEIZO HINO, *Isle of Dreams.*
ALDOUS HUXLEY, *Antic Hay.*
Crome Yellow.
Point Counter Point.
Those Barren Leaves.
Time Must Have a Stop.
MIKHAIL IOSSEL AND JEFF PARKER, EDS.,
Amerika: Russian Writers View the United States.
GERT JONKE, *The Distant Sound.*
Geometric Regional Novel.

Homage to Czerny.
The System of Vienna.
JACQUES JOUET, *Mountain R.*
Savage.
CHARLES JULIET, *Conversations with Samuel Beckett and Bram van Velde.*
MIEKO KANAI, *The Word Book.*
YORAM KANIUK, *Life on Sandpaper.*
HUGH KENNER, *The Counterfeiters.*
Flaubert, Joyce and Beckett: The Stoic Comedians.
Joyce's Voices.
DANILO KIŠ, *Garden, Ashes.*
A Tomb for Boris Davidovich.
ANITA KONKKA, *A Fool's Paradise.*
GEORGE KONRÁD, *The City Builder.*
TADEUSZ KONWICKI, *A Minor Apocalypse.*
The Polish Complex.
MENIS KOUMANDAREAS, *Koula.*
ELAINE KRAF, *The Princess of 72nd Street.*
JIM KRUSOE, *Iceland.*
EWA KURYLUK, *Century 21.*
EMILIO LASCANO TEGUI, *On Elegance While Sleeping.*
ERIC LAURRENT, *Do Not Touch.*
VIOLETTE LEDUC, *La Bâtarde.*
SUZANNE JILL LEVINE, *The Subversive Scribe: Translating Latin American Fiction.*
DEBORAH LEVY, *Billy and Girl.*
Pillow Talk in Europe and Other Places.
JOSÉ LEZAMA LIMA, *Paradiso.*
ROSA LIKSOM, *Dark Paradise.*
OSMAN LINS, *Avalovara.*
The Queen of the Prisons of Greece.
ALF MAC LOCHLAINN,
The Corpus in the Library.
Out of Focus.
RON LOEWINSOHN, *Magnetic Field(s).*
BRIAN LYNCH, *The Winner of Sorrow.*
D. KEITH MANO, *Take Five.*
MICHELINE AHARONIAN MARCOM,
The Mirror in the Well.
BEN MARCUS,
The Age of Wire and String.
WALLACE MARKFIELD,
Teitlebaum's Window.
To an Early Grave.
DAVID MARKSON, *Reader's Block.*
Springer's Progress.
Wittgenstein's Mistress.
CAROLE MASO, *AVA.*
LADISLAV MATEJKA AND KRYSTYNA POMORSKA, EDS.,
Readings in Russian Poetics: Formalist and Structuralist Views.
HARRY MATHEWS,
The Case of the Persevering Maltese: Collected Essays.
Cigarettes.
The Conversions.
The Human Country: New and Collected Stories.
The Journalist.
